For Dave and Kupper Airport's South Side Lounge regulars.

AN AIRFIELD MYSTERY

AS THE PROP TURNS

PENNY THOMAS

Published by Hallard Press LLC.
www.HallardPress.com 352.460.6099

Library of Congress Control Number: 2023919920

Publisher's Cataloging-in-Publication data

Names: Thomas, Penny, author.
Title: As the prop turns / Penny Thomas.
Series: An Airfield Mystery
Description: Hallard Press LLC: Hallard Press LLC, 2023
Identifiers: LCCN: 2023919920 | ISBN: 978-1-962326-20-9 (hardcover) | 978-1-962326-09-4 (paperback) | 978-1-962326-10-0 (ebook)
Subjects: LCSH Airports--Fiction. | Amateur sleuths--Fiction. | Mystery fiction. | BISAC FICTION / Mystery & Detective / Cozy / General | FICTION / Mystery & Detective / Women Sleuths
Classification: LCC PS3620 .H46 A7 2023 | DDC 813.6--dc23

ISBN: 978-1-962326-20-9 (hardcover)
ISBN: 978-1-962326-09-4 (Paperback)
ISBN: 978-1-962326-10-0 (ebook)

CHAPTER 1

The phone chirping in my ear added another level to my annoyance, which was already in the red zone. I'd spent three hours battling the traffic from Manhattan for this early morning appointment with our marriage counselor in New Jersey. And now I'd have to reschedule because my no-good, woman-chasing pilot husband hadn't shown up and wasn't answering his phone. I'd had to take a day off work to get to this small town where I'd spent the past three years of married life.

The chirping stopped. *Yo, this is Joe...* I hung up on his over-long voicemail greeting. If I left another message, I might look needy, which would be bad for my hoped-for divorce.

I stopped pacing and turned to face the waiting counselor. Mustering my calmest, sweetest voice, I said, "I guess that soon-to-be ex-husband of mine forgot we were meeting this morning."

"We still have twenty-five minutes left of the appointment, Mrs. Tomei. We can talk about your conflict. We could explore your use of the phrase, soon-to-be-ex. What are your expectations about this counseling process?" She settled her ample frame into her enormous, butter-yellow leather chair and made some sit-down and relax motions with her hands. I thought her smile had a touch of eager anticipation.

I suppressed my glower at her pleasure. "No thanks. I want to have a face-to-face confrontation, I mean discussion, with Joe. No offense, but I don't want to air my woes and grievances without him hearing them. He didn't want to come to this meeting. He said we could work it out alone. Yeah, right! Work it out. This is how he works things out. He avoids the issues. I could murder him." I could feel myself slipping deeper into my pissed-off mode. I took a deep, calming breath. Letting this lawyer-mandated marriage counselor see me losing control would not do. "I'm calling him again." I speed dialed.

"Hello. Who's this?" The muffled voice on the other end of the phone didn't sound quite right. Had I caught Joe in bed again with that flight instructor, Maria? And why didn't he recognize my number?

"It's me. Who are you with? Where are you? Why didn't you come to the counselor's? If you want to fix this marriage, you'd better get your butt over here." I sucked in oxygen and waited for a fabrication of lies worthy of Pinocchio to spew out over the airways.

Instead, a vaguely familiar voice said, "Fiona? Is that you? This is Chuck Boyd."

Now, Boyd was Joe's flying friend, but that didn't give him the license to answer Joe's phone. What was going on? "Boyd? Why are you on Joe's line?"

"There's been an accident. Joe is hurt."

Boyd's words hung in the space between my ears and brain. There was an unexpected tightness in my chest. All of a sudden, my knees felt wobbly. I collapsed into the nearest chair.

"How bad?" My voice came out all squeaky.

"Bad. The EMTs are on their way. You'd better get here."

"Where?"

"On the airfield. On the west end of the runway, by the ultra-light strip. I gotta go; here comes the ambulance." Boyd hung up.

"Oh my God. My husband is hurt." I gathered up my bag, struggled from the depths of my chair, and headed for the door.

The counselor bleated a few questions at me and made a futile attempt to get out of her chair. I fled, fearful that if she succeeded in separating herself from the butter-yellow leather, she would clutch me to her ample bosom in a consoling embrace.

I broke my personal best running record as I raced across the parking lot. I could hear the distant wail of an ambulance over my screeching tires as I two-wheeled it onto the county road leading to the airfield. *What the hell was Joe doing at the ultra-light strip? He promised he'd make the counselor appointment. Had he been flying? Why didn't I ask Boyd if it was an airplane, car, or motorcycle crash?*

I ignored the two *Stop* signs on the three-mile route to the airfield. After what seemed an eternity, I turned up the access road and raced past the flight school. I skidded through the perennially open security gate and onto the apron. At the far end of the runway, I could see the flashing lights of the emergency vehicles. They acted as a beacon, urging me on. I tore across the apron, past the flight school and rental fleet of Cessnas, and headed towards the runway. I was just about to cross when the years of training by Joe and other airfield denizens brought me to a sudden halt. Their mantra, *check for any aircraft in the pattern,* filtered into my brain. I scanned the skies for any imminent takeoffs or landings for this small, no-control-tower, general aviation airfield. There was nothing in the bright blue October sky. No aircraft were in the pattern, nor were there any on the shimmering runway. I crossed and roared up the main taxiway. My tires squealed in protest as I swerved off the blacktop onto the unpaved ultra-light field access road. Skidding on the cinders, I overcompensated and zig-zagged at high speed towards the lights.

Three police cars, an ambulance, a fire truck, and a knot of people obscured the accident scene, so I couldn't see what vehicle Joe had crashed. I bumped off the cinders onto the grass and came to a stop. For a moment, I couldn't move. The adrenaline that had borne me this far faded. I did not want to get out and face the results of the accident. My hands were frozen to the steering wheel. Was it a good or bad thing that all the activity was a little apart from the ambulance? I couldn't tell by sitting here. I had to get out of my safe cocoon and go and see. A few uniforms turned around to look when I slammed the car door shut. A police officer peeled off from the crowd and approached me with his arms wide, stopping me from getting any closer. I didn't recognize him. He hadn't been on the force when I left town six months ago.

"You can't come any further," said the young officer.

I dodged to one side, and he feinted left, blocking my move, and we ended up nose-to-nose. Under any other circumstances, it would have been funny. I took a step back to reassess my position, and out of the corner of my eye, I saw someone break away from the crowd and walk quickly toward me.

"Fiona, you made it." Boyd put his arm around my shoulders.

"He won't let me through." I pointed accusingly at the officer, who merely shrugged and stood his ground.

"Let her through. She's his wife." Peter Ward, retired cop and, pre-divorce proceedings, my flight instructor, was one step behind Boyd. "The EMTs are with him. Come on."

The cop gave up his position in the face of the two well-known town residents. As I got closer, the wall of people parted before me. I saw the blanket-covered body on the ground and two EMTs being busy over it. The blanket wasn't pulled up to cover his face. *He's still alive.* I knelt and put my hand on Joe's forehead. He looked peaceful, lying there with his eyes closed. I couldn't see any blood.

"Hey, Joe," I whispered. I couldn't think of anything to say. *I love you,* just didn't seem appropriate right now. And neither did, *What the hell happened?* So, I just held his head and wished he'd open his eyes. My wish came true. Joe's baby blues fluttered open, and he stared straight at me. His lips moved. I thought I heard the word *Water.* I lowered my ear to his lips, "What?"

"Water." This time, I heard the word clearly and so did one of the medics nearby.

"We can't give him water, Ma'am, until we know what internal injuries he has."

"I'll get you some water later, Joe," I whispered.

He struggled a bit and said, "No. Water, water…" and then his eyes closed.

The EMTs started doing something around the lower half of his body. I stroked his curly, dark hair. I thought back on what had attracted me to him first. Was it those black curls or his blue eyes? The contrast was startling, and when you added in that wry smile from his generous lips, the combination was fatal to any woman who crossed his path. And, believe me, a lot of women came into his orbit.

"Ma'am, you have to move." The voice startled me out of my reverie.

The EMTs were ready to lift Joe onto a gurney. Reluctantly, I took my fingers out of Joe's curls and stood up. Carefully, they half wheeled and half carried him over the bumpy turf to the ambulance.

I felt a touch on my arm and turned to see Peter. He had tears in his eyes. "Go with him Fiona, I'll follow in my car."

The notion that Peter expected me to go with Joe threw me for a moment. Didn't he know we were getting a divorce? I noticed the police, EMTs, and some of the airfield people were watching me. Did they know? Were they waiting to see if I got into the ambulance? Had Joe shared with them our marital woes? It was a small town, and Joe knew everybody. Heck, most of the people standing around had gone to his high school. Many graduated with him. They must know, and I didn't care. I hitched up my too-short and too-tight suit skirt and clambered up the ambulance step.

Then I heard the scream.

"Let me through. Joe, Joe, where are you? What happened?"

I twisted around on the top step to look. The mass of blue uniforms swayed and moved aside to reveal my nemesis and arch enemy, part-time waitress at Mama Rosa's, and part-time instructor at the flight school, Maria Avernus. She was also, in my opinion, the airfield slut and the reason for my impending divorce. She was running towards the ambulance, crying and sobbing. The watching population moved back as if distancing themselves from the scene. I froze to the top step of the ambulance, trying to squash down the urge to fling myself at her and scratch her eyes out.

"Get in and sit down." Peter reached up, placed his hands on my butt and shoved hard. He slammed the door behind me, hitting me in the rear. I heard him rap sharply on the door as a signal to move on. The ambulance rumbled into life and lurched across the lumpy, dry grass. I looked through the little window and watched Maria chasing after us. If I were a better person, I'd feel sorry for her. But I wasn't. I hoped she'd trip on one of the many gopher mounds that dotted the grass.

CHUCK BOYD and Peter Ward sat silently on either side of me on the cold, hard orange plastic chairs lined up against the gray wall of the emergency waiting room. A handful of uniformed and two plain-clothes police stood at the farthest corner. They didn't talk but kept shooting looks over to me under cover of changing positions. What were they thinking? The only sound was the ticking of a wall clock marking, minute by minute, the interminable passage of time.

A distant door slammed in the silence, making me jump. Footsteps drummed over the linoleum, getting louder and closer. I heard a shout, "Joe? Joe? Where is he?" The waiting room door burst open, and Maria came to a halt at the entrance. I watched her eyes sweep the room and come to a stop when she saw me. She pointed her finger at me. "You! Why are you here? Joe belongs to me. You have no busi-ness here." She took a couple of steps towards me, her hands forming claws aimed straight at my face.

For a nano-second, nobody else moved. Then, we all reacted as one body. I stood up, ready to do battle. This was my chance to inflict bodily harm on this marriage destroyer. Boyd and Peter leaped to their feet. The cops unfroze from their huddle and moved towards me.

Somebody swore. Another said, "We've got to get her out of here." The cops rushed to Maria, swept her up in their midst and hustled her out of the room. The mass of bodies created a bottleneck at the door. I couldn't see her, but I could hear her. "Let me go. Is he alright? I have a right to be here. She doesn't." Her voice became fainter as the mass of blue uniforms propelled her down the hall. Peter and Boyd, being the furthest away from the exit, gave up the struggle and came back to take up their self-appointed positions of guarding me from the world's evils.

"Don't worry. The guys will take care of her," Boyd said.

"You've got to feel sorry for her." Peter peered through the window of the now-shut door.

"Why? She was sleeping with my husband. I hate her." The sound of the venom in my voice shocked me. And, judging by the intake of breath, it also shocked my two bodyguards. Without another word, they resumed their positions on the orange plastic chairs.

The wall clock ticked on.

This time the footsteps came from the emergency room side of the double doors. They were slow and measured and got louder. I couldn't take my eyes off the doors. The steps came to a stop, but the door didn't move. I could see a shape through the round porthole. It stayed still for a couple of heartbeats. For some reason I felt I had to stand up to meet whoever it was. Peter and Boyd also stood and flanked me. Mesmerized, I watched the doors swing slowly open.

"Mrs. Tomei?" The person in green scrubs looked at me. I nodded, unable to trust my voice. "I'm so very sorry. There wasn't anything we could do."

I didn't hear the rest. All the pent-up anger I'd been hoarding for months evaporated. My legs trembled and turned rubbery. The room went into a kaleidoscope of green scrubs, gray walls, and orange chairs. I groped for a seat and collapsed onto it. Joe, the man I once loved, was gone. I couldn't breathe. I heard sobs coming in big gulping gasps and realized they came from deep inside me. Tears poured down my cheeks and snot dripped off my nose. I searched futilely in my pocket for a tissue.

Boyd dug in his pocket and held out a rag. "Here, use this. It's sort of clean."

Ignoring the black stains and faint smell of engine oil, I thankfully blew my nose and scrubbed my eyes.

"Would you like to see him?" Green Scrubs' voice penetrated my fog.

For a second I hesitated. Did I want to see the shell of my one-time lover, friend and husband? I felt the urge to preserve my memory of him as a vibrant person. I was afraid of dead bodies. I thought of my last vision of him on the gurney. That would remain with me always. Did I want a worse one? I opened my mouth to say *No*. There was a commotion by the door. I looked up to see the cops, *sans* Maria, filing in. Everyone's eyes were upon me. I could sense them all—Peter, Boyd, the green scrubs person, and the blue uniforms—waiting for me to do something. Small-town New Jersey people took body-viewing very seriously, it indicated respect for the dead and the living. These rather cold and calculating thoughts calmed me. I had no choice. I nodded, then followed Green Scrubs through the swinging doors.

Inside, I saw everything in high definition and slow motion. Shining steel glinted in the harsh overhead light. The smell of antiseptic was overpowering. The soft murmurs and rustlings from three other Green Scrubs working around the periphery of the room stopped when I moved in on the stark white sheet-shrouded body in the center of the room.

Someone gently folded back the top of the shroud and I looked down into the face of my husband. It was surprisingly serene. As if he didn't know what had happened. He looked like he was sleeping. I moved closer and gently smoothed back a lock of his hair. "Oh Joe, I'm so sorry. Please forgive me for being mad at you." Then, damn it, the tears started again. A hand touched my elbow. I shrugged off whoever it was at my side and raised the dirty, oil-smeared rag to wipe away my tears. I didn't want to have to say the final goodbye. Waves of exhaustion flooded my body, but I had to do it. "Goodbye, Joe." I touched the white shroud about where his heart once beat, then brought my hand up to my heart. It was over. I wasn't sure what to do next.

"Come on. You're not needed here anymore. I'll drive you wherever you want to go." It was Peter's voice. I turned to look at him and remembered past scenes when my marriage was young. Summer evenings, after a good day of flying, a group of pilots and aircraft enthusiasts gathered by the maintenance hangar and swapped tall tales. Peter was the best story-teller. He regaled us with hilarious sagas of his time with the police. He joined the force straight out of school. Did his twenty years and retired to take up an equally stressful occupation of teaching people to fly. It seemed this small town in New Jersey had more than its share of drug dealing, murders, thefts, kidnappings and extortion. Funny, on the surface it looked just like a neat little commuter town, but underneath, according to Peter, it was a hot-bed of intrigue. Joe laughed the loudest and egged Peter on to tell more stories.

I liked Peter then, and I liked him now with his offer to take me away from this place. But I didn't know where I wanted to go. The drive to Manhattan takes an hour and a half in good traffic.

"If I go back to my apartment in The City, I'll only have to come back here tomorrow, won't I?"

"Probably. The police will want to ask you some questions. Maybe you should go to your in-laws."

"Oh no! I forgot about them. Did someone call them? Where are they?" Some time had passed since the accident. They should have been here by now. They only lived minutes from the airfield.

"I called them. They were in the Bronx, shopping," Boyd said.

This astonished me. "Why so far away?"

"Arthur Street," Peter said by way of explanation.

Then I got it. Arthur Street was the last bastion of the Italian immigrant population in New York City. Joe had taken me there a few times. Specialty food shops filled with cheese, sausage, bread, pastries, fish and Italian produce jostled for space among family-run restaurants. The area was redolent with appetite producing aromas from Genoa to Sicily. The Tomeis had relatives there and periodically would visit to stock up on foodstuff and family gossip. I was born in the Bronx, but on the wrong side according to my in-laws. I came from the Woodland section, where all the Irish lived. This geographic separation was the basis of much animosity between me and Joe's family.

"Do you want to wait for them here?" Peter asked.

"Oh God, no. I can't see them now." Peter and Boyd raised their eyebrows at my outburst but I resisted the urge to explain.

I needed to be cool and calm to deal with the inevitable hysteria and hostility my mother-in-law, Rosa Tomei, would direct at me. I was sure she would find some way to blame me for the loss of her baby. She didn't want Joe to marry me. She had someone else in mind for him. Someone from the old neighborhood. She believed I influenced Joe to keep the airfield property as an airfield and not sell out to developers. She blamed me for Joe's passion for flying, even though he got his pilot's license years before we got together. My mind went back to the day I laid eyes on Joe Tomei three and half years ago. It was a beautiful January day and I was on my first visit to what I later found out to be a 'general aviation airfield.' Back then, I didn't even know they existed. All I knew about aviation were places like Newark and JFK and large passenger aircraft that took you on vacation.

No, I couldn't face Mama Rosa today.

"Get me out of here. I'll go to Joe's." Peter and Boyd were probably in Joe's confidence and knew I was filing for divorce and that Joe still lived in 'our' house. "I'll call my room-mate, Jessica. She'll come out and stay with me."

CHAPTER 2

Peter insisted on staying with me until Jessica's train arrived so I wouldn't be alone. He said he'd go and pick her up. This suited me. I needed answers to all the questions swirling in my brain.

"What happened this morning?" I might as well get him started at the beginning.

"I'm not sure. I was driving to the ultralight field, where they lay out the banners for towing pick-up, when I heard an engine cough and splutter. Then it cut out. It's a bad thing when the engine quits as you dive down to pick up a banner. He didn't stand a chance."

My ears pricked up at the word banner. It didn't make sense. Joe hated banner towing.

"Why was he towing a banner?"

"I don't know why. Ask Boyd. It's his operation, and he asked me to check the banner rig for a tow that morning, I got his message too late." Peter slumped in his chair and rubbed his eyes. The poor guy looked bereft. He'd lost a lifelong, close friend. I was over my initial, and surprising to me, overwhelming grief. I was sad, but the image of Maria at the crash site and in the emergency room, kept my emotions in check. In reality, I'd lost Joe six months ago when I caught him in our bed with Maria.

A thought popped into my head, did Maria have a key to this house and would she try to get in to harass me? I shelved this thought for the time being, but I was more than ready to take that slut on. First, I needed to know what happened today.

I eyed Peter. It would be kind of me to let him alone with his thoughts. But I quickly dismissed the idea. I wanted more answers. "Why did he fly? He knew he had to meet me today. There wasn't enough time to take a banner and fly it up and down the shore before coming to the counselor's office."

"Fiona, I just don't know. All I saw was his plunge to the ground." Peter thumbed on the TV, tuned into the Weather Channel, and locked his eyes on the muted screen filled with isobars, wind arrows, and the prevailing jet stream.

I gave up on the questions for the time being. I had to think. It didn't make sense. Joe didn't like anything to do with banners or the airplanes that towed them. He refused to let anyone use our Super Cub to drag banner advertisements over the crowded beaches and suburbia of New Jersey. Our Super Cub had a towing hitch, but Joe said the weight of a banner or glider burned out engines. Joe would fly anything with a wing, but he didn't like banner towing. 'It was boring,' he said. 'Flying up and down the shore with the engine roaring so loud you can't think. You gotta make sure you're low enough so sunbathers can read that the gecko company has the best car insurance. That Milly and John are getting married. And Sam's Crab House has a blowout special of all you can eat.' My mind skittered back and forth, trying to come up with a reason for Joe's death, but I got no answers. And Peter wasn't giving out any at the moment.

Finally, it was time for the train to arrive, and I could pack Peter off to meet it and bring Jessica back. Just in case there were lots of the early train commuters getting off, I gave him a detailed description of her. Black hair, styled in an asymmetrical jag cut, probably wearing her trademark Jones New York, size two, pant-suit. To make double sure he couldn't miss her, I added the information that she'd most likely be carrying her favorite Kate Spade Wise Owl tote and clutch. He looked bewildered at all this information, but before I could elaborate, and add the probability she'd also be wearing her treasured red Jimmy Choos, he jumped into his Ford pick-up truck and drove off. I was alone in a too-silent house.

I looked around the living room. Joe hadn't changed a thing over the six months we'd been apart. All the little feminine touches I'd added to his bachelor house were still there. Mind you, the jewel-toned cushions I'd bought to soften up the look of the black Naugahyde living room set that pre-dated me by many years, were scrunched up in one corner of the couch. Joe must have fallen asleep watching TV. I swallowed the lump that rose in my throat at the thought of him snoozing through his favorite NCIS show.

I checked out the bedroom. Typically, Joe hadn't made the bed. My eyes lit on the photo by 'his' side of the bed. It had been taken on our honeymoon in Italy. We'd escaped from the legions of his third and fourth cousins—once or twice removed—and were checking out the little towns that clung to the coast. We'd asked a passing tourist to take this photo. Joe stood behind me and rested his chin on my head. I hated it when he did that, it made me feel so small. But now I really wanted to feel the familiar weight of him. His blue eyes stared at me out of the picture, partially obscured by the same dark lock of hair I'd brushed away from his forehead earlier today. I gave myself another minute to gaze at the photo and remember a happier time, then shook my head. *Enough already, stop moping.*

The bedroom wasn't in too bad a shape. A little messy in a male sort of way. I picked up a pile of dirty T-shirts. Should I throw them into the garbage or the laundry hamper? The hamper won out. Tossing them in the garbage would have been too final. A bit like throwing Joe himself into the trash. *I'll give them to Goodwill when they're clean.* I turned my attention to the bed. We only had one spare room and Jessica would sleep there. That left me to sleep again in 'our' bed. Did I want to do that? Did I want clean bedding or used ones with Joe's scent still on them? In my maudlin state, I favored Joe's scent and went to straighten up the rumpled sheets.

Then I found it.

Underneath the pillow on 'my' side of the bed was a scrunched-up piece of black silk. I teased the wad open. "Ewwww!"

Disgust and curiosity fought for dominance. Curiosity won, I spread the thin fabric out, and my finger slipped through a hole. I dropped the black silk, and all the tender thoughts I'd been having about Joe and our past disappeared. I was so not going to sleep in these sheets. They had to be disinfected. I pulled off the top sheet, and let out a shriek. Another black, silky bundle nestled at the bottom of the bed. I scooped it off the linens and it opened up. And so did my mouth. Lace-edged holes were where nipples should be winked at me. This was too much. "Peek-a-boo bras and crotch-less panties! I'll kill the bastard." Then I remembered he was already dead.

Luckily, there was nobody around to hear my screams of distaste and murderous mutterings as I got down to getting rid of the evidence of Joe's nocturnal playtime. I tore the plastic off Joe's dry cleaning and wrapped the offending garments in the bag and stuffed them into Joe's dresser drawer. I planned to confront Maria with them in the very near future. Then I scrubbed my hands clean of any possible alien bodily fluids.

Taking deep calming breaths, I faced the bed. Everything needed to be sterilized. I stripped it of everything — even the mattress pad — and stuffed it all in the washer with the hottest water temperature available. No female flight instructor's DNA was going to survive this washing. I threw all the towels in for good measure, who knew where they had been. Still breathing heavily with indignation and exertion, I made up the bed with fresh linens. I was just about to head into the bathroom to scrub all contamination from the porcelain when the doorbell stopped my fervent quest to rid the place of all things Joe and Maria.

Jessica dropped her bags on the porch. "Oh honey. How are you holding up? I'm so sorry."

I was impressed at her show of concern. Jessica never lets her Kate Spades touch the ground. She hugged me so tightly I couldn't breathe.

"I'm so glad you made it. Thanks for coming out here." I pulled her into the house, leaving Peter and her bags on the porch. "I don't want to stay in this house alone. Too many memories. You'll never believe what I found. That S.O.B...."

"Ladies, I hate to interrupt, but I got a call from my buddy at the police station. The Tomeis and Maria are hysterical over Joe and pointing fingers at you, Fiona." Peter had followed us in and set Jessica's bags by the front door.

"Me? What did I do?" Righteous anger boiled up. First Maria inexplicably blamed me for Joe's death and now his family was doing the same.

"They're saying you caused Joe's death."

"How's that possible? I wasn't even there."

"They're saying you called in at the flight school this morning and asked about the Super Cub."

"So? I wanted to see if it was in flying condition."

"Why did you want to know that?"

"It's been a long time since I flew, and I thought I might get you to take me up later on for a lesson."

"Why didn't you call me first?"

I did not like the tone of Peter's voice. "I lost your number."

"They could've given it to you."

"I hung up before Frank in the flight school could give it to me."

"Why?"

"A State Trooper pulled up alongside me. I didn't want a ticket." I hated to admit that I was driving and dialing to a retired cop. "What's going on, Peter? You're beginning to sound like a police officer."

"Old habits die hard. Maria and the Tomeis have lived here a long time, and they have some pull in the town. They're angry, and they're hounding Detective John Masters to find someone to take responsibility for the death of their loved one."

"Well, it wasn't me. You said Joe's engine quit. That's what is responsible. It was an accident."

"We don't know that. The National Transportation Safety Board should be investigating, but they can't and I'm not sure the police have the skills."

"Why not?" I asked.

"None of the town's police know anything about airplanes."

"No, I mean, why can't the NTSB investigate?"

Jessica cut in before Peter could answer, "Because they're part of the federal system and that's shut down. We've got a lawsuit at work that involves the NTSB, and it's come to a screeching halt because the idiots in Washington are arguing over the budget and sequestration. Government agencies are not working."

"My buddy said they're asking for some mechanics to come over from Princeton Airport to take a look at the airplane. See if they can figure out why it crashed. Meanwhile, the Tomeis are out for blood. If not yours, someone's. They want answers," Peter added.

"I want answers too. I want to know why Joe was banner towing instead of meeting me at the counselor's office." I put my arm on Jessica's and moved her towards the living room.

Peter followed. "I know you want answers, and so do I. But I don't know why Joe was flying instead of Boyd."

"Then ask Boyd. Call him now."

"Okay, I will." Peter pulled his phone from his pocket, but before he could punch in the number, it started buzzing. "It's my buddy at the police station again. Hello?" He retreated to the front porch. I strained to hear what he was saying but failed.

Jessica took my hand and squeezed tight. "Let it go for now. You look all in. I brought some wine. We'll sit and chill, then deal with this in the morning."

Peter came back in and said, "I've got to go now. The police said they'd be around tomorrow morning." He turned to go without elaborating on what his friend had told him. I wanted to ask him, but a wave of fatigue swept over me. I'd had enough of men for a while. I wanted to drink some wine and talk to a sympathetic female. Jessica fit the bill. And I had a sneaking suspicion Peter had enough of me and was using any excuse to get out of here.

I saw him to the front door, thanked him for his help, and shut the door on the ugly world outside.

"Any ideas where Joe put the wine opener?" Jessica called out.

"If it isn't in the drawer by the stove, I don't know. I haven't been in this place for six months. No telling where he put things. He was a slob around the house. But neat at the airfield." I joined her in the kitchen, pulled open a couple of drawers, and rummaged around for the corkscrew. The idea of a nice glass of Merlot was very appealing. "Here it is. I wonder why he put it in the food baggie drawer, and where did he put the baggies?"

Wine poured; we took our glasses out to the back deck. It was a bit chilly out there in the early fall shade, but I didn't want to sit on the front porch in the warmth of the setting sun as it might give the neighbors an excuse to stop by and ask questions disguised as condolences. I was under no illusion that the news hadn't reached every adult in town.

"Tell me, what did you find that I wouldn't believe?" Jessica asked as she raised her glass to her lips.

It took two glasses of wine to get the black lace crotch-less panties and peek-a-boo bra saga off my chest. At the end of my righteous rant, Jessica had the nerve to laugh. I twisted in my deck chair to glare at her. "It isn't funny. Those things looked like something you buy in an *Adults Only* store in those decrepit old strip malls."

"How do you know about those stores? You're way too uptight to know what goes on in there." Jessica snorted into her wine glass. She wasn't doing a good job of hiding her amusement.

Despite my indignation, I started to giggle. It must have been the influence of the wine, as I was still outraged by the black underwear. "You only know my New York Business Woman persona. I've seen the dark and skanky insides of those stores." Ignoring Jessica's attempt at wide-eyed shock at lost innocence, I sucked the last drops of wine from my glass and reached for the bottle. Sadly, it was empty.

"Is that where you met Joe?"

"No, it wasn't." I thought back to our first meeting, three and a half years ago. "That story will take a lot more wine and I'm getting cold."

"I brought more than one bottle. Let's go inside."

I gathered up our empty glasses and led the way into the now dark living room. Jessica pulled another bottle from her capacious overnight bag and proceeded to open it.

With our glasses replenished and feet comfortably propped on the coffee table, I turned to Jessica, raised my glass and toasted, "Here's to Joe, the best-looking woman chaser I know…I mean, knew."

Jessica raised her glass back at me, took a sip then asked, "So, if it wasn't at a sex shop, where did you meet? You never told me that."

"I guess I was too busy complaining about the horrendous state of my marriage to talk about the good times at the beginning." I took a deep breath and dove into a past I'd rather forget.

"My office had a Christmas raffle. The kind where you buy a bunch of tickets and put them into the basket with the prize you want. The only thing that interested me was a spa day. But for some reason, and to this day I don't know why I did it, I put half my tickets in a bucket that announced, *A birds-eye view of New York and New Jersey at three thousand feet with your own private pilot.* I must have thought it would be fun."

"I'd have put all my tickets in the day-spa. I hear Atlantic City has a great one. Let's go sometime." Jessica topped up our wine glasses.

"Yes, lets. I should have put all my tickets in that bucket. I do love apricot scrubs."

"I love the mud baths, but they wreak havoc with your hair. Mind you, that's a good excuse for a scalp and hair follicle treatment and a new do.

"Jessica sipped meditatively on her drink. "But I interrupt. I'm guessing you won the airplane ride."

"Right."

"Wow. Weren't you scared?"

"Yes, and frozen. Like an idiot, I decided to cash it in on Martin Luther King Day. It was one of those fabulous sunny winter days and the snow was still on the ground. I thought it would be great to take aerial pictures of white fields and use them as my Christmas card. I'd send them to all my old high school friends who send me pictures of their kids dressed in red and green velvet and posing in front of a merrily burning *Ye Olde Yule Log.*

"You sound bitter."

"Not bitter, just disillusioned with love and life. I hate those cards. It's as if those ex-cheerleaders are saying, *nah, nah, nah, look what a lovely family I have.*"

"But you had a great career in advertising and you lived in New York City."

"I know, but my mom was always on my case about getting married, settling down, and having kids." I checked my wine level. It was getting low.

"Is this where Joe comes in? Did you marry him to please your mom?"

"In hindsight, I guess so. But he was such a gorgeous specimen of manhood, I couldn't resist." I drained my glass and held it out for a refill. Jessica obliged. "Back to my raffle prize. I got a train out to the wilds of New Jersey and then a taxi to this little airfield. Did you know that there are nearly five thousand small airfields all over the United States? It's part of something called General Aviation."

"How do you know this stuff?"

"I looked it up after I met Joe. There are more than six-hundred thousand pilots in this country and a quarter of a million general aviation airplanes. And that's not counting the passenger and cargo airlines, or the military."

"Why on earth would you research and remember all this?" Jessica frowned.

"I wanted to impress him. It stuck in my memory, like a lot of other stuff."

"Like what?"

"Like how pilots do this thing called a pre-flight every time they fly. They walk around their airplane and wiggle all the moving parts. They check to see if a bird or insect has built a nest in the airplane. And they check the fuel for any water."

"Why the nests and water thing?"

"I quote Joe; *Foreign objects can cause an engine stall and a possible crash.* Joe was paranoid about his pre-flights, especially water in his fuel. Anyhow, back to my flight. It was fabulous. I fell in love with flying and I fell in love with Joe. We got married a few months later. And now it's all over." I could feel the tears coming, so I swigged too much wine and choked.

The feint worked. Jessica only saw the tears from my coughing. She thumped me on the back and announced, "I'm hungry, are you? We should eat something. Maybe order in. I'm guessing there isn't anything in this bachelor house."

"I haven't looked, but you might be wrong. Joe and I ate Mama Rosa's leftovers mostly. She sent round care packages nearly every day. I bet there's some sort of pasta dish in the fridge."

"Who is Mama Rosa? I've not heard you mention that name."

"My mother-in-law. She owns the Italian restaurant next to the airfield." I hadn't told Jessica much about my married life. We met in the gym soon after I found out about Joe's infidelity. We hit it off immediately and by coincidence she was looking for a roommate at the moment when I knew I couldn't stay in the same house as Joe any longer. I moved in with her a week later.

"Yum, a good rich Italian meal sounds wonderful. I haven't eaten pasta in ages." Jessica patted her almost flat stomach. "You stay here and I'll go and forage for food." She flipped her fingers in a goodbye and headed for the kitchen.

I leaned back on the Naugahyde and closed my eyes Was it only this morning that my life had been on its new, six-month old, normal track? It seemed like an eternity. My stomach rumbled. I rubbed it, liking the feel of the newly forming muscles. Five days a week at the gym were paying off. You'd think I wouldn't want any food after the day's events. But my soy latte was hours ago and in a different state.

I HAD JUST FINISHED MOPPING up the last of Mama Rosa's marinara sauce over linguine with the heel of garlic bread when the front door burst open. We were sitting at the breakfast bar with our backs to the living room and front door. Our uncoordinated swivels on our stools brought us face-to-face. It took us a second to sort our tangled knees out and focus on the door. By that time George Tomei, Joe's elder brother, Mama Rosa's number one son, manager of the family restaurant, and hater of all things Fiona, had stormed into the living room.

"What the hell did you do to my brother?" George pointed his finger at me.

"I didn't do anything George. He did it all by himself."

"You should be the one dead, not Joe. Ever since you came into this family, you've been trouble. You caused his distraction. He wasn't paying attention to the airplane because of the divorce. In my book that makes it your fault."

Now George and the rest of the Tomei clan hated the fact that Joe loved aviation and owned a time and money-sucking airfield. They alternated between blaming me or the airfield for the neglect of his duties to the family restaurant.

George moved in closer and stood over me. I should have got down from my stool when he first burst in, now I was backed against the bar with this giant looming over me. Threat emanated from every inch of his substantial, some might say obese, frame.

"That's ridiculous, George, and you know it. Joe was big on airplane safety, no matter what distractions he might have had. And I was making the divorce easy for him."

"He didn't want a divorce. Tomeis don't divorce even if they married wrong. The Tomei women stick with their men." George glared at me.

"The Tomei women are stupid then if they stick with a man who is having affairs. I caught him with Maria. Who knows how many others he bonked? Maybe you know." I eased off my stool with as much grace as I could muster with George in my space. This was sort of a mistake. George loomed even taller now I was standing. Being short has its disadvantages. One of them is spending most of one's life not seeing eye-to-eye with most people. But I didn't care. I needed to move out of his orbit and his disgusting droplets of spittle. I drew myself up to my full five feet. There was no way this in-law, the one I disliked most, was going to intimidate me.

"Get out of my house." And, just in case he didn't get the message, I pointed to the still open front door.

"This is the Tomei house, not yours. It's always belonged to the family. We gave it to Joe, not you. You're not welcome here." George didn't move.

Deep breaths Fiona, don't let this ape make you lose your cool. "I'm still a Tomei, and I've every right to be here."

"Introduce me, darling. I don't think I've met this person." Jessica's voice, overly sweet and polite, fell onto momentary silence.

Mentally thanking Jessica for the interruption, I ushered her forward. "Jessica, this is Joe's older brother, George. He runs the restaurant Mama Rosa's. George, this is my friend Jessica Feinstein." I love following the social mores of a formal introduction. It can be so civilizing.

I watched George carefully, and sure enough, he reacted to Jessica's elegance and poise. She cut a spectacular figure, matching George inch for inch. His eyes widened. I wished I could read his calculating, nasty mind. Was he weighing his chances at impressing Jessica or throttling me?

His eyes flickered from her to me. "Enough chit chat. You get out of this house now or else."

"Or else what?" Now I was breathing heavily and ready for battle.

Jessica eased in between us and faced George, "That sounds like a threat." She turned to me and asked, "Should we call the police, darling?" Her voice was still calm and sweet.

"It might be a good idea. George, are you threatening us?"

His eyes narrowed and he chewed his under-lip. I'd seen that look before. George was sifting through his options.

Now I hate long silences, and this one went on for a couple of heartbeats longer than I liked. So, I opened my mouth, "Anyhow, I'm going to stay and give Joe the funeral he deserves."

Big mistake.

George sucked in a breath. "No. The family is doing the funeral. Stay out of it."

Jessica put her hand on my arm. I knew I should shut up, but like an idiot I didn't. "I am the wife. I get to decide the funeral."

I hadn't a clue what to do for funeral arrangements. This was mercifully a chore I'd never had to do. And, I'd just as soon let someone take over. But George's threats made me determined to get involved somehow. Just to rub his nose in it.

"Mama will do it all." He said this with a finality I'm sure he thought I couldn't argue with as Mama Rosa ruled all the Tomei men. But I wasn't about to give in. I'd faced down Mama Rosa a couple of times. I hadn't won, but I had tried. I still have the mental scars to prove it.

"I'm doing it."

"You won't have time. I heard the police want to question you," George said.

I didn't doubt that George had heard this. He had friends everywhere in the town.

"Of course they want to question Fiona. They'll want to question everyone." Jessica worked in a law office with a heavy criminal client base. Some might call them Mafia. She knew about these things. "But questioning doesn't mean she's guilty of anything."

George turned to look at her. "What business is all of this to you? Why are you here?" I guess he'd given up on the thought of flattering Jessica.

"To protect Fiona from bullies like you. Now get out before we call the police." Her polite façade fell away and she jabbed her finger in George's chest.

I held my breath. What would he do? He looked from me to Jessica. I swear I could hear the gears clanking and grinding in his pea-size brain mulling over whether he could pop us both on the nose now or not. I thought it would look good in the local press. *Brother of slain pilot beats up grieving widow and friend.* He must have made up his mind that he was out-maneuvered for the time being. He clenched and unclenched his hands, shook his head, muttered something that didn't sound nice and turned on his heel and left. The front door slammed shut behind him hard enough to make the house shake. I ran to double lock the door after him. The dead bolt was stiff, but I got it to work. People didn't usually lock their doors in this town.

"That was unpleasant." Jessica sank onto the couch. "Was Joe like his brother?

"No. Joe was a charmer. As a menopause baby, his parents gave him anything he wanted. George always acted nasty around me. He didn't like his baby brother either. Mom and pop Tomei doted on Joe, and George was jealous. They used to give Joe money from the restaurant when he ran short, which was often."

I took my wine from the bar and joined her. "Thanks again for being here." I clinked my glass to Jessica's and raised it in a toast. "We won that round."

"I think this is only the beginning. Your friend Peter also said the police wanted to talk to you. I wonder why they haven't already got in touch."

"They're being nice to a new widow." I answered. Hoping it was true.

"The police are never considerate." Jessica took another sip of wine. "Let's go over what happened today after you left the apartment at that unearthly early hour."

I thought over the long day. "Our appointment was for ten o'clock. It usually takes two hours to drive via the Turnpike. But I don't have E-ZPass and I didn't have any change for tolls, so I left earlier and used local roads. Traffic was light and I got here about nine-thirty. It was a beautiful day and I guess I missed flying. I'd been taking lessons with Peter before I left Joe. I swung by the flight school to get his number and book a lesson."

"You told Peter you had called the flight school."

"I did that as well. But I didn't finish the call because of the trooper on my tail, so I stopped by. I had the time."

"Did you book a lesson?'

"No. There wasn't anyone at the desk when I walked in so I left."

"Why didn't you wait?"

"Now you're sounding like a cop," I said.

"They'll ask you the same questions. It's best you know the right answers."

"I saw Maria outside by the airplanes. I didn't want to have to talk to my husband's girlfriend. So, I scribbled a note for Peter and left."

"Sounds reasonable. I can't see anything to be worried about. Now, let's drink and watch a movie." Jessica held out her glass.

I reached for the wine bottle. It was empty.

"There's more in my bag." The woman had come prepared.

CHAPTER 3

buried my head under the pillows, hoping to muffle out the intrusive ringing. It didn't work. I could still hear it through three layers of bedding. I groped for my cell phone on the bedside table and pressed it to my ear.

"Hello?" Nobody answered. But the ringing went on. I opened one eye then shut it quickly to block out the bright sunlight streaming in from the crack in the window blinds. My head hurt. I regretted the final bottle of wine Jessica and I had polished off last night. I peeked at the clock radio, it read ten fifteen. The ringing continued. There was nothing for it, I had to keep my eyes open. My cell showed I'd missed three calls from the same local number. But there was nothing coming in right now. Where was that noise coming from? Pounding on wood now joined the ringing. My wine fuddled brain finally registered that someone was at the front door and wanted to get in. *Please don't let it be George again.* I had to make the din stop before my head exploded. I pulled Joe's terry-cloth robe over his old T-shirt I'd slept in, padded bare-foot out the bedroom, and bumped into Jessica in the hall.

"There's someone at the door," I said, just in case she missed the obvious. She looked as hung-over as I felt.

"I can hear. Tell them to go away and leave us in peace." She turned back into her bedroom.

I nodded my head in agreement. Big mistake. The violent motion started a new cluster of throbbing near my left temple. I made a half-hearted turn back into my bedroom, but the door pounding increased with the added notes of, "It's the police, Mrs. Tomei. Open the door."

Police? Oh God. The neighbors must be having a field day hearing all this. I couldn't open the door dressed, or should I say undressed, like this. I tottered up to the door and whispered at it. "Please go away. I can't see you right now."

"I'm sorry, Mrs. Tomei, we need to ask you some questions."

"Can we do it later, when I'm dressed?" I croaked.

I heard some talking on the other side, but couldn't make out the words. Sounded like more than two people. I wished I had a little peephole in the door like I have in The City to look out and see who was there. I prayed it wasn't a posse of police outside on my porch. I'd never live it down in the neighborhood.

"We can come in and wait until you get dressed."

I looked around the living room. It was a testament to an evening of drowning my sorrows. Last night, after recapping the day's events, we decided we needed cheering up and turned on the TV. Serendipitously, *Mama Mia!* was playing. I seem to remember dancing on the coffee table at one point in the evening. The results of our evening antics were all around. The place was a mess. Wine bottles on the floor and glasses tipped over on the coffee table. Dirty dinner plates with the congealing remnants of Mama Rosa's linguine and marinara sauce clinging to the porcelain were still on the breakfast bar. The throw cushions were scattered over the couch, chairs and floor. Draped over the back of the seats were six or seven brightly colored, long silk scarves I'd dug out from the box I meant to have taken to Goodwill a year ago. I cracked a smile at the remnants of our rousing rendition of *Dancing Queen*. Eat your hearts out Meryl Streep, Julie Walters and Christine Baranski. However, the scene wasn't quite in line with how a grieving widow should behave.

"No, you can't come in now. Look…I'll come down to the station as soon as I get cleaned up. Say in an hour or two?"

More muffled consultations from behind the door. I was so glad I'd double locked it last night after George's visit. Short of breaking it down with a battering ram, nobody could get through it.

"Okay, Mrs. Tomei. You come down to the station. Ask for Detective John Masters."

Footsteps retreated down the porch steps and car doors slammed shut. Then an engine started up. I twitched aside the front window drapes and peeked out to see a retreating squad car. The two elderly sisters who lived across the street were peering out their front door. They must be peeing in their pants with delight at the activity going on.

"Jessica, get dressed. We're going to the police station." The sound of water running in the bathroom was the only answer. *Good move Jessica, you got in there first.* A nice hot shower would clear my head, but now I'd have to wait. Not for the first time I wished this old, small, ranch-style house had a second bathroom.

I'd better find something to wear. I rummaged around the closet and drawers. Jessica had brought me a change of underwear, but that was all. I put clothes shopping on my mental to-do list for the day. The *Goodwill* box provided a faded pair of jeans and an old white tee. Those and one of Joe's sweaters draped around my shoulders, would have to do.

"I'm out of the bathroom." Jessica called.

My turn at last. The ice-cold water shocked the breath out of me. I'd forgotten that Joe's father, and ever hopeful amateur handyman, had plumbed the shower wrong. The hot faucet delivered cold water. I added this to my growing list of reasons I didn't like the Tomeis. Finally, the steaming hot water needled into my body. I remembered now how good a multi-head spa shower at full power felt, even if it was plumbed wrong. I stood under the streaming water until I ran the tank dry of hot. Feeling refreshed and ready to face the day I toweled off and blew my hair into some semblance of order.

T̲HE̲ S̲MELL̲ of coffee and toast greeted me. "God bless you Jessica, please tell me there is some cream in the fridge."

"Yes, and the 'sell by' date is in the future. Who was at the door?" Jessica opened the fridge door.

"The police. They were ready to storm the place."

"This place is full of surprises. First police then a cold shower."

"Sorry about that. I forgot about that little water trap." I poured myself a mug and took a sip. "This coffee is heaven."

"What did the police want?" Jessica nibbled on her toast.

I grabbed a piece of toast and spread it with *Nutella*, another relic of my marriage. I didn't dare look at this 'sell by' date. Joe hated the stuff. I could eat it by the spoonful. I wondered why he hadn't thrown it out. A brief thought that Maria might have dipped her spoon in it flashed through my mind, but the lure of chocolate and hazelnut won over that repulsive prospect and I bit into the toast with relish.

"Detective Masters sent his boys to bring me in for questioning." I wondered if I meant this as a joke or not. "Will you come with me?"

"Of course I will. I said so last night. You'll need some sort of moral support. We can tell them I'm your advisor, then they'll let me in."

"I can bring anyone I want with me, I'm not under interrogation. I'll tell them you're my best friend...and you are. You're my only friend at the moment." I got a little teary eyed when I said this. A mouthful of *Nutella* chased away the pathos along with the eye-roll from Jessica.

"You never know with the police. I remember one client..." Jessica was off on one of her long legal stories. She'd been with a law firm of one kind or another, since college. I told her she should have gone to law school. She had more than eighteen years' experience in the business. Why stay at the paralegal level? Her answer was she had to choose to either study for the bar or party. She chose to party. "...so, that's why I think you should get a lawyer." This statement broke my train of thought and jerked me back to the present.

I was just about to ask her to repeat herself when the doorbell rang accompanied by some hard knocking. "Don't tell me the police are back." I went to the door prepared to give Detective Masters and his minions a tongue-lashing for his impatience. The two hours I told him we'd be there by weren't up yet. But the man standing on the porch was definitely not a police officer. He was short and skinny and clad in an impossibly shiny suit. The word zoot-suit sprang to mind. My father had one of those. I found it when I cleaned out my parent's house after they died. The little man's dark hair was slicked back and it glinted in the late morning sun. He flashed a smile at me — again with the shining. Those teeth would make any dentist proud. I disliked him on sight.

"Mrs. Tomei?"

I was getting tired of that name. I planned to change it after the divorce. "Yes."

"I am sorry for your loss. Please accept my condolences. My name is Demetri Balasi, I am a business partner of your husband."

This was news to me. Joe had always been against partners. Said it diluted his property and authority.

"What kind of business partner?"

"Perhaps I can come in and we can discuss it?" Balasi moved an inch closer.

I stood my ground. "I can't talk now; I have an appointment."

"I understand, Mrs. Tomei. There must be so many things to take care of. If you need my help you just have to ask." The words were sincere, but I sensed the sentiment wasn't. I felt he was just going through the motions. "Please let me explain the situation, it won't take long." He edged in another inch and I swear I could feel his minted breath waft over me.

I so wanted to slam my door on him, but short of being obnoxious, I couldn't think of any reason why I shouldn't let him in. And I kind of wanted to know more about this partnership. I stepped aside to admit him.

"Are the police annoying you again?" Jessica called from the kitchen.

"Not the police. This is Demetri Balasi. He says he's Joe's business partner."

Jessica eased off the stool and came to check out our latest visitor. Balasi took one look at her and puffed out his chest. His eyes shone. This man was all around impossibly shiny, to the point of being oily. But I could see why he had this look of admiration, one could even call it lust, on his face. Jessica was, as usual, impeccably dressed in a silver-gray pants suit. Her black hair lay sleek against her head and her make-up was flawless. I don't know how the woman does it. There was no indication of the night of debauchery we'd had, she was glorious. Then, I swear, Balasi oozed forward, took her hand and started to raise it to his lips. My jaw dropped.

Jessica snatched her hand away out of danger and took two steps back. "Interesting. Fiona, did you know Joe had a partner?" She looked at me and took a step back out of Balasi's orbit.

"No, I didn't. Why don't you tell me all about this partnership Mr. Balasi?" I tried to make my voice sweet and charming. However, my words come out rude and curt. Never mind. I wanted to know what Joe had been up to. A partnership would have affected my divorce share.

"I don't want to trouble you lovely ladies with all the boring business details at such a sorrowful time as this. I only came by to offer my condolences and clear up a little matter."

"No trouble. We're very interested." Jessica managed to make her voice sweet and charming. I had to learn to do this.

"Are you perhaps related to Mr. or Mrs. Tomei?" Balasi was matching Jessica's sweetness with saccharine.

"No, neither. I am however Mrs. Tomei's advisor, especially in legal matters." She beamed at him. I swear I could hear her cheeks crack. I knew the signs. Jessica was on a roll and ready to fight.

Balasi fidgeted. He eyed Jessica for a beat longer than necessary. I couldn't read the expression in his eyes, but I got the distinct sense it was no longer lustful. "I really don't want to trouble you. This will only take a minute. I have a few papers that Joe neglected to sign and there is some urgency in the matter. Perhaps Mrs. Tomei can do the honors?"

"I'm sure she would be pleased to, after I've looked them over. You can leave them safely with me, Mr. Balasi." Jessica held out her hand for the papers.

"As I said, there is some urgency. We can clear this up in a few seconds if Mrs. Tomei will sign right here." He ignored Jessica's extended hand and pointed to a line on the paper clutched tightly in his hand.

I looked from one to another. I was rather enjoying the scene. I loved seeing Jessica at her iciest efficiency. Neither was willing to cede ground. The silence stretched on, interrupted only by the ticking of the wall clock. Then the strident clamor of a phone broke the spell. I jumped, and so did the other two. Our heads swiveled as one to look at the faux rotary phone by the front door. I rushed over and picked it up, wondering who would be calling me on the land line. "Hello?"

"Detective John Masters here. Can you give me an idea of when you're coming to the station?"

"It's the police," I announced to the room.

Balasi's head jerked around to look at me, his eyes widened. "This can wait. I'll see you again." He quickly stuffed the papers into his folder, slithered out the door and eased it carefully shut behind him.

I looked at Jessica and she looked at me. We raised our eyebrows in sync. "That was strange," she said.

I agreed and turned again to the phone. "We're just leaving now Detective Masters. We should only be five or ten minutes." I hung up, picked up my purse and fished around for my car keys. They weren't in there. I checked the ceramic bowl on the breakfast bar. But my old spot to dump out pocket and purse contents was empty except for a few coins and a thumb drive.

The doorbell interrupted my search. It was getting like Grand Central Station in this house. I flung open the door, ready to give whoever was standing there a blast of pent up frustration.

Peter stood there, smiling, "Thought you might need a ride to get your car or anywhere else you need to go."

Then I remembered. My car was still at the airfield, at the accident site. Six months of living in The City and using public transport had severed the umbilical cord between this suburban woman and her car. I opted for the police station, if only to get Masters off my back. I'd figure out a way to get my car later.

"Thanks Peter, you're a sweetie." Jessica flashed one of her traffic stopping smiles at him and folded her long legs into the back seat. I could see she had another fan. He peeled out of my driveway so fast I had to clutch the passenger door handle to stop myself falling into his lap. *Show off.*

I straightened up and fastened my seat belt. "Peter, do you know anything about Joe having a partner?"

"No, why do you ask?"

"A slick little guy came around and said he was Joe's partner. I forget his name, Greek or something."

"Demetri Balasi," Jessica said from the back seat.

Peter's eyes left the road and locked on mine. "That son of a bitch, what's he doing sniffing around you?"

"Who is he?"

"He's Maria's cousin. He has an air cargo operation in South Florida. He keeps flying into the airfield and meeting with Joe."

"Maria's cousin!" I inhaled sharply. I had to keep calm. *That slime-bag is related to the slut.*

"What's this partnership he talked about?" Jessica leaned over the front seat and pressed her hand on my shoulder and squeezed. I knew she shared my outrage.

"I don't know what his deal is but I bet it isn't legit. I don't know how Joe got caught up in his net, but you want to avoid him. Next time he bothers you, call me. I'll get rid of that little freak." Peter pulled up in front of the police station. "I'll see what I can do about getting your car from the airfield."

Then he actually got out of the driver's seat and opened the passenger door for Jessica. I had to open my own door. I waited impatiently for our shining knight to finish his chivalry bit hoping to find out more about Balasi and Peter's suspicions. But a police car pulled up and honked at us. Peter hopped in his car and pulled away from the 'No standing' zone. I watched his brake lights go on as he two-wheeled it into the parking lot. Jessica had this effect on guys. She made them act like teenagers.

THE DESK OFFICER looked up from his busywork, did the usual male double-take and body scan of Jessica. She'd just added another member to her fan club. I've gotten used to the effect she has on men and no longer resent the fact that I become invisible when she's with me.

After a round of 'who are you and what do you want?' we were escorted towards the rear of the police station to meet Detective Masters. He was another new cop in town. Seemed there'd been some new hires since I left. I assumed it was because of Jessica's fabulous looks that he didn't put up a fight when I promptly informed him that she was coming into the interrogation room with me.

"What makes you think you're going to be interrogated?" He asked.

"The way you sent your boys around to pound on my door at the crack of dawn and then hounded me on the phone before I was ready to leave my house."

Masters lips twitched. I couldn't make up my mind if he was annoyed or laughing at me. Mind you, it could have been a nervous tic being he was standing right next to Jessica and I'm sure he was getting a full olfactory blast of her *Obsession*.

"Ten o'clock in the morning isn't the crack of dawn."

I inclined my head, conceding his point. *Touché Mr. Detective, but remember, I'm the grieving widow, I'm entitled to lie in bed all morning.* "Let's get this interrogation started. I've a lot to do today." I hoped I sounded brisk and efficient. I had only one big thing I should do today, buy clothes. Oh yes, there was more. I remembered I had to face my in-laws and organize a funeral. It was going to be a busy day.

Masters ushered us into a small room with an oak table and four faux-leather covered chairs. I couldn't see a one-way mirror and the table didn't have a steel bar bolted on it for handcuffing prisoners. This was a conference room. It seemed I didn't warrant an interrogation room. I wasn't sure whether to be relieved or disappointed. We took our seats and Masters flipped open his notebook.

"Mrs. Tomei, I'm sorry for your loss." He paused for a moment to let the condolences take effect. "Now, let's get some background. How long were you and Joe married?"

"Three years, two months and five days."

Masters's eyebrows shot up. I couldn't tell if he was surprised at the length of time or that I had it down to the day. I could tell him the hours and the minutes if he wanted. I remembered that day well. Joe was late. His excuse was …

Masters interrupted my train of thought, "I understand you two were divorcing. Tell me, who instigated the proceedings?"

Now this was a little too personal for my taste and I didn't see how it had anything to do with the accident. Masters might be new to the area, but surely, he'd be in on the gossip surrounding Joe and Maria. I debated whether to ignore the question. I eyed the man sitting on the other side of the table. He was quite good looking in a stern, military way. Dark blonde hair, cut a little too short for my taste. Clean shaven and not an ounce of fat on his medium height body. His eyebrows raised in question over smoky gray eyes. I decided to play nice and answer. "I was."

"Why?"

"What has this got to do with Joe's accident?"

"We have reason to believe it might not be an accident."

Master's words hung in the stuffy conference room air. I heard Jessica suck in her breath. I couldn't make sense of his statement. If it wasn't an accident, then what? A picture of Joe's white-sheet shrouded body flashed in my brain. Was this man intimating that Joe had killed himself? How could he think that? The concept that my fun-loving, full of life, husband would commit suicide was outrageous.

"That's impossible," I said into the long silence.

Jessica reached over and held my hand. I stared at Masters in horror and waited for an explanation.

"We don't have all the facts yet, Mrs. Tomei. But preliminary investigation indicates it the crash was premeditated."

"What did you find?" Jessica asked the question burning in my mind.

"It's too early to say. The Princeton mechanics haven't turned in a full report yet," Masters sat back in his chair, narrowed his eyes, and furrowed his brow for a long moment. Then he sat forward, shuffled through his papers and looked at me. "You called the airfield in the morning Mrs. Tomei. Why?"

"I wanted to go flying."

"Oh, so you know about airplanes."

"Yes. Some. Not much."

"Do you know how to pre-flight an aircraft?"

"Of course I do. It's the first thing I learned. Why do you want to know all this?"

Masters passed over my question and started another line. "Where were you yesterday morning, Mrs. Tomei? Say between six and nine?"

"In bed then driving here." I was answering automatically. All I could think of was Joe being desperate enough to kill himself. No wonder the Tomeis were out for my blood.

"Where in bed?"

"Our apartment in Manhattan."

"Joe and you had an apartment in The City?"

"No. Jessica's and mine. Actually, it is Jessica's, she's letting me stay with her until the…"

"Don't say anything more. You should have a lawyer." Jessica interrupted me.

"Why do you think she needs a lawyer, Miss…? I'm sorry, I forgot your name." The warm, admiring look wasn't in Master's eyes right now when he glanced at her.

Jessica drew herself to her full sitting height, which was just as impressive as her standing height. "She needs a lawyer because now your line of questioning sounds as if you suspect her of something. Fiona, don't say anything more. Why did you say it wasn't an accident?" Jessica and Masters stared at each other.

I wondered who would blink first. Masters did, but it seemed that didn't mean he caved. He flipped over a page in his notebook and turned to me, "What time did you leave the apartment?"

"I don't remember. In enough time to get here for my ten o'clock appointment with the counselor," I snapped at Masters.

"Can't you see she's upset?" Jessica turned to me. "Let's get out of here. I want to call my boss and see about legal representation."

"Don't worry, Mrs. Tomei. We can check your E-ZPass records for your journey on the Turnpike." Masters smiled as he said this. Was he nuts to think I was worried about remembering the time I left the apartment? I didn't have anything to hide. I was worried about Joe's state of mind before he died. Anyhow, I didn't use the Turnpike. I hate it and the Garden State Parkway. I know it takes longer, but I use local roads whenever I can. And they don't need E-ZPass.

I opened my mouth to mention this to Masters when Jessica grabbed me by the elbow and hissed in my ear, "Not another word. Let's go." She must have remembered what I told her yesterday about my route.

Jessica didn't say anything until we were outside the police station. "Isn't that Peter with your car?" Still holding onto my arm, she strode towards it, saying, "As soon as we get safely into the car, I'm calling you a lawyer."

"I don't need one."

"I didn't like the tone of that detective's questioning. You need representation." Jessica liked to sound lawyerly at times. "And you were at the airfield before your marriage counselor's appointment. We don't know if the police know about that."

I was just about to ask why I would need a lawyer when people thought Joe might have committed suicide when we reached my car. Peter and a cop were deep in conversation and didn't see us approach.

The two of them were studying an evidence bag in the cop's hand. I glanced at the contents. It was a box of zip-lock baggies. The cop whispered something to Peter and they both looked at me.

"What's going on?" I asked.

"I found these under your front passenger seat," Peter answered.

"That's strange. I wonder how they got there," I said.

"Are they yours Ma'am?" the cop asked.

"No. I don't like that brand, and I wouldn't keep baggies in my car."

The two men exchanged looks. Then, without a word, the cop turned and walked to the police station and disappeared inside.

"What's the big deal about the baggies?" Jessica had noticed the silent communication between the two guys.

Peter leaned against my car. He had the same exhausted, defeated look about him as yesterday. "The Princeton mechanics found remnants of a plastic baggie by the aircraft's cracked open gas tank."

"I still don't understand what you're getting at."

Peter's hesitated, then said, "Seems someone might have put a bag like this full of water in Joe's gas tank. That's possibly why his airplane went down. We think it was sabotage."

The implication of Peter's words hit me. The wine and marinara sauce over linguine of the night before rose to my throat. I made it to the bushes in two big steps and deposited everything I'd eaten or drunk in the past twenty-four hours onto the boxwood. I dry-heaved and gasped for breath...someone had murdered Joe. He hadn't committed suicide.

I felt an arm come across my shoulders and a hand appeared with a tissue. I grabbed it and wiped my mouth. Jessica gently pulled me up.

"Explain the significance of plastic baggies in a gas tank." Jessica directed her glare and question to the now white-faced Peter.

"When water gets into aircraft fuel, it works its way to the carburetor and the engine ceases to function. For obvious reasons, this isn't good when flying and that's why pilots check for water before taking off. But, if you put water in a plastic bag and insert the bag in the fuel tank, that water won't show up immediately. But, after a short time, the fuel will melt the plastic and water will leak into the fuel. Then the engine stops." Peter wiped his hand over his face as if to erase the image he'd just conjured up.

"Oh my God," Jessica whispered. Her grip around my shoulders tightened. I was thankful for that as I'd lost all strength in my legs. "Let's get out of here before Masters gets those baggies and calls you back in. You're in no condition to face him again. I'm driving." She held her hand out for the keys.

Peter handed them over. "He knows about the baggies. We called it in. But yes, get Fiona away from here, she doesn't look well."

He was right, I wasn't well...there was still some remnants of yesterday clamoring to leave my body.

Peter took over Jessica's position of support and ushered me into the passenger seat. He gently closed the door. I saw Jessica say something to him and he answered her. She frowned in reply and said something back. He replied. I wanted to know what they were saying but the windows were up. I opened the door and they stopped talking. Jessica flipped her fingers in goodbye and got into the car.

"What were you two talking about?" I asked.

Jessica adjusted the seat and rear-view mirror before answering, "I wanted to know if the police had any suspects."

"Do they?"

"He couldn't, or wouldn't, tell me. But he did say he saw George Tomei nosing around Joe's stuff in the maintenance hangar when he drove by in your car."

This statement quickly cleared up the remnants of my nausea. I was angry now. I was mad at whoever was responsible for Joe's death and at my nosy brother-in-law. I wanted to hurt someone and George was as good a target as any. "Take me to the airfield. I'm going to find out who killed Joe."

"Leave it to the police, Fiona."

"No. You heard Masters. He thinks I caused Joe's accident."

Jessica sat in silence for a moment. Then, with a sharp nod of her head, started the car. "Let's go find ourselves a saboteur."

"And a murderer." I settled into my seat.

CHAPTER 4

directed Jessica past Mama Rosa's Restaurant on the corner of the airfield access road and Main Street. Wanting to check out the restaurant, but not wanting to be seen by any Tomeis or locals lurking in the parking lot, I managed to simultaneously slide down in the seat and crane my neck to stare as Jessica carefully navigated the many potholes. It was open and doing a brisk business. You'd have thought they'd be closed to mourn their loss, but that would mean losing money, and the Tomeis loved money about all else. I chided myself for my bitchy thoughts. Maybe the hired staff were the only ones in there working away. There were more cars outside than I remembered there being for a Friday lunchtime crowd. I bet half the people were there just to find out information about the crash and to ghoulishly gawk at the family of the deceased.

"I wonder who's cooking if George is engaged in snooping around Joe's office and hangar." I rotated my head a couple of times to get the crick out of my neck.

"George cooks? I thought your mother-in-law did."

"She supervises now. George does most of the work. He griped at Joe about it. Wanted him to help out with the cooking."

"Oh, you mean that delicious sauce was made by that obnoxious hulk? I wish I'd known. I wouldn't have mopped up the last bits." Jessica said.

I laughed at her look of disgust. "Joe might have made it. He was a good cook too."

We swung past the flight school. I did the slide down in the seat and crane my neck maneuver again as I wasn't ready to talk to or be seen by anyone just yet. A couple of people were standing under the wing of a Cessna. It looked like they were doing a pre-flight. I debated about going in to use the bathroom. My mouth was still thick with vomit residue. The mints Jessica had fished out of her bag helped a bit, but a good rinse with water would be even better. However, the thought of facing the curiosity of the office staff, and the possibility of Maria being in there, won over my wish for a mouth gargle, face wash, and pee.

A few yards further on the access road was the aircraft owner's entrance to the airfield itself. The security gate was open, just like it was yesterday when I tore through it to say goodbye to Joe. I could tell by the way Jessica squeezed my knee that she knew what I was thinking.

She hesitated at the gate and looked out over the apron and runway. "Which way?"

"Turn right and go down that little taxiway. See the big hangar at the end? That's Joe's."

The hangar man door was ajar. Did Joe leave it like that? Surely someone would have come over and secured it last night. Or was George still in there?

Jessica must have had the same thought. "Be careful. I'm not sure I can stare down that goliath again."

I gently pushed on the man door and cursed the shriek of rusty hinges. Now whoever was in the office in the back would know they had visitors.

Giving up any idea of sneaking up on George and catching him in heaven knows what act, I called out, "Hello, anyone in there?"

My voice echoed back from the cavernous space. Nobody replied. George was either lurking in the office or hiding among the stacks of spare parts and tools. Or he could have left. Taking a deep breath, I stepped over the high threshold. It took a moment for my eyes to adjust from the bright sunshine outside to the darkness of the empty hangar. Empty? It should be filled with an airplane.

"Where's the Super Cub?"

"Where's the what?" Jessica was so close behind me I could feel her breath on the top of my head.

"The Super Cub, our airplane."

"What does it look like?"

"Single-engine, high wing, tandem seats with a red fuselage."

"Like I know what you mean by that description."

"There are quite a few on the airfield. We passed a couple parked outside the flight school. Chuck Boyd's banner towing operation uses them."

"Maybe it's outside. Didn't you say you wanted to go flying yesterday? Joe might have taken it out so it was easy for you to use."

"He might have got it down by the fuel pumps. If he was in a good mood, he'd have fueled it for me. Mind you, he didn't really like me flying it. He wanted me to take lessons in the school's crappy Cessnas."

"Why's that?"

"I guess he thought I might damage it. He rebuilt it from the frame up. It's a nice airplane, very pretty."

"Did he forbid you to fly it?"

"No, he couldn't do that. The registration is in my name. Something about keeping it safe from liens. He just complained every time I flew it."

"Maybe George moved it out of the way of whatever he was looking for."

"I doubt it. George hung around here a lot. But it was more for the company than the airplanes. He wouldn't open the big doors and push it out. That takes effort, and George doesn't like exertion. It's probably on the other side by the pumps." We were now at the far end of the hangar and in Joe's office. It was empty.

"Phew, it smells a bit of dead mice in here." Jessica wrinkled her nose.

The tiny office looked undisturbed. But, as I hadn't been in it for some months, what did I know? Joe was very meticulous, dead mice notwithstanding. The sight of the neat, white labels on the filing cabinets brought a lump to my throat. I'd made those labels some time ago. I squatted down in front of the filing cabinet and pulled open the *Miscellaneous Business* drawer. I wasn't sure what I was looking for. I'd take anything—an explanation for Joe's death or more on Demetri Balasi and his business dealings. I thumbed through precisely alphabetized files associated with running a business. These labels were also hauntingly familiar. I'd created those folders when we first got married and I helped Joe run the airfield. Towards the back my fingers flicked on a tab labeled *Real Estate*. This wasn't one of my labels. The words were cut from a printed piece—like a magazine, letterhead, or business card. The hanging folder was a different brand. This wasn't Joe's work. He liked everything matching. What was Joe doing investing in real estate? The papers I'd glanced at in Balasi's hands were more of an aviation partnership, not real estate. I pulled the folder out, but it was empty. I wasn't going to get any answers here.

"Hey, Jessica." My knees cracked as I stood up. Note to self; more squats at the gym needed in future.

She turned from her examination of the three-ring binders on the shelf.

"Come help me look for the contents of this folder. You take these drawers and look for any papers to do with real estate or that creep Demetri's business plan. I'm going to search his desk." I settled into Joe's battered and lumpy office chair.

I felt a bit mean giving Jessica the manicure-destroying job of flipping through files, but I didn't want her, or anyone for that matter, searching through Joe's desk. I was on the hunt for any compromising pictures of Maria and Joe, and any nude ones of me taken in our happier days. There was also the possibility that Joe had some girlie magazines and condoms in his drawers. I felt the need, I don't know why, to censor any humiliating finds.

I found nothing compromising.

I sat back in Joe's chair and looked at Jessica sitting on the floor in front of the filing cabinets. She must have forgotten about the dead mouse and the possibility of the existence of its live cousins. The smell wasn't so noticeable now. We must have gotten used to it. "Did you find anything?"

"No. Do you think that brother-in-law of yours took the contents?"

"I can't think of anyone else who would. But what and why? Let's go. I need the ladies' room and I want to see where Joe put the Super Cub."

We locked up with my set of keys. Funny the stuff one keeps. I never thought I'd be out here again after I left Joe, but I had hung onto the keys. The lock resisted my key for a moment as if protesting a long absence. A touch of WD40 would soon fix that. The draft divorce settlement my lawyer had drawn up gave me half the value of the airfield, but it was to stay in Joe's name. He had to come up with the cash to give me. Maybe that's why he wanted us to work out our problems ourselves. He'd never had any cash while we were together. And I doubt he had any more while we were apart.

"No, don't go that way. Cross over the runway." I pointed right. Jessica was still doing the driving and had turned left towards the flight school. I still wasn't ready to face those people in there, even though it was close by. "I'll use the bathroom on the south side and then we can go and talk to Chuck Boyd about why Joe was banner towing for him."

We headed off on the apron. I made Jessica stop before she crossed the runway. The place was eerily quiet for a sunny and windless day. I wondered if it was still closed to air traffic because of the accident. Probably not, Joe had come down on the grass in the ultra-light field on the southwestern side, far away from the runway and out of sight of the hangars. The feds don't like closing airfields up for long. I mentioned this to Jessica as we scanned the skies for any airplanes in the landing pattern.

"Peter said the feds weren't involved yet. And they won't be until the idiots in Washington get over their snit and re-open the government."

"Maybe the police have the place closed up." I said.

"Would they have the authority to close a federal entity up? I doubt it." I could hear Jessica's brain clicking through the legal aspects of this.

"I guess it doesn't matter either way. Come on, there's nothing in the sky. Turn left by the fuel pumps towards the line of hangars over there."

The only door open along the double line of hangars was the bathroom door. The cold water felt good on my face. Unfortunately, there weren't any towels so I had to let the sun and air dry me off. I was refreshed and ready to face the next hurdle.

"Chuck Boyd isn't here. That's strange, he never closes his doors during the day." I looked around, not sure what to do next. Then I remembered I hadn't found the Super Cub. "Come on, let's drive up the line of airplanes on the tie-downs."

"Isn't that close to where you said Joe crashed?" Jessica hesitated before getting into the car.

"He went down past the airplanes. Over there, behind that little rise in the grass. You can't see it from here. But I do want to go out there."

"Do you think that's a good idea? It'll be upsetting." Jessica still hadn't got into the driver's seat.

I contemplated going around the car, taking the keys from her, and driving myself. But, to tell the truth, I still felt shaky. Maybe my hangover hadn't gone.

"Look, the Tomeis say I had something to do with the crash. The police found plastic bags in my car. Peter's wondering why I didn't call him about flying yesterday. Nobody likes or trusts me. I have to get some answers and maybe the crash scene has something. I'd like to see it. All I saw yesterday was Joe on the stretcher. I want to see what killed him." I could hear my voice rising a bit and I was alarmed at how close to tears I was getting. These emotional ups and downs had to stop if I was going to find out why Joe had to die and who was responsible.

Jessica must have sensed this because she came around the car and put her arms around me. "Come on sweetie, don't cry. Well go out there. I'll drive."

My heart beat faster as we slowly cruised along the tie-down line of single engine aircraft. My mind flitted between dread of the approaching crash site and hope that Joe's Super Cub would materialize amongst the Cessnas and Pipers lining either side of the taxiway, props pointing to the sky in defiance of any bird wanting to roost there. We reached the last one and I looked back along the line of shining aircraft. Had I missed ours? But the familiar red livery wasn't visible. Maybe it was on the other side of the runway in the new tie-down area. I'd check that later.

"Where to?" Jessica stopped the car at the intersection of the runway.

"Go along that path by the cemetery." I pointed to the crushed cinder path that ran alongside the fence.

"That's spooky, having a cemetery next to an airfield." Jessica said as we bumped along the pitted road.

"I hadn't thought of that. At least the residents don't complain about the noise of airplanes taking off and landing." I laughed in spite of my nervousness of what was around the bend of the path.

"Good point. Do the people on the north side complain?" I could tell Jessica was making small talk to stave off my obvious jitters about what was ahead at the ultra-light field. So, I dove into the saga of the airfield and the homeowners. But before I could get into a righteous rant, Jessica sneezed.

"I'm sorry. It's the Golden Rod. I'm allergic." She sniffed back another sneeze.

"I've got some tissues somewhere." I turned in my seat to grab them off the back seat. It took me some stretching and reaching, but finally I snagged the box and turned to face forward. Then I saw it—a mangled mass of aluminum and the all too familiar red fuselage. "Oh my God. Stop. It's Joe's airplane."

I jumped out of the car before Jessica brought it to a complete halt and ran over to the wreckage. I couldn't see the registration number. Maybe I was wrong. Maybe Boyd had bought another Super Cub since I was last out here. Maybe…I moved closer and ducked under the yellow police tape staked around the perimeter. I prayed it wasn't Joe's airplane. If it was, then the crash made even less sense. Then I saw my emergency blanket and all doubts disappeared. The bright purples, blues and greens of the perfectly hideous afghan my mother had so lovingly crocheted for my college dorm room many years ago was incongruously still neatly folded on the remains of the passenger seat. Joe loved that afghan, even though it clashed with the Super Cub's livery.

I sank to the ground and put my head into my hands. I gagged on the odor of spilled aviation gasoline that rose from the earth. Alternating between dry heaves and breathing in noxious fumes, I tried to think, to make sense of it all. My mind ticked over with too many questions. Why was Joe flying our airplane? Yes, it did have a tow hook so it was mechanically possible to tow a banner. But Joe hated doing this, especially with his airplane. In the back of my mind, I'd assumed that Boyd was the target as I thought it was his airplane that crashed. But now it was clear, Joe was the intended victim. The sabotage was now very personal. I wished I had one of the airsick bags tucked behind the pilot's seat. The grass absorbed the absolute last remnants of yesterday and today's intake.

"You alright?" Jessica was standing over me.

"No, I'm not. This is the Super Cub I was looking for. It's Joe's and mine. I don't know why he was flying it and not one of Boyd's." As I said these words, I started to get angry at everything and everyone. I was pissed off at the Tomeis, the police, Peter, Boyd and Joe. Yes, I wanted out of the marriage, but not this way. I didn't want Joe to die doing something he loved and was good at. And I sure didn't want him to die while destroying the airplane that he and I had spent so many happy hours renovating. "It's not fair."

"I know, Sweetie. But it happened. Now we're going to fix it." Jessica pulled me to my feet, gave me a hug, and said, "First off, we take pictures."

"Why? The police must have a full set of photos."

"It's always good to have our own in case we need evidence."

"Evidence of what?"

"We don't know yet. But we're going to find out." Jessica was in her legal persona. She was very thorough with her picture-taking. She shot every angle. I couldn't figure out what we'd do with these photos, but the very act of doing something helped me take my mind off all the questions swirling around in my brain. Photos taken; we left the scene.

"Let's go back past Boyd's place again. Maybe he's there now and can give us some answers." I ceded all driving privileges to Jessica for the day, I didn't trust my emotions at this point.

CHAPTER 5

huck Boyd's hangar door was now open to reveal a red and white Super Cub with its cowling off. Various engine parts lay on the ground. Not a good sign for a man with a one-airplane banner towing operation and a sunny autumn weekend coming up.

"Hello. Boyd. Are you there?" I called out the minute Jessica turned off the car engine. I was relieved and excited to see signs of habitation. Maybe now I'd get some answers.

"In here." A voice called out from the tiny room at the back of the hangar that he called his office. I picked my way over the tools and parts scattered along my path. Boyd was not a neat freak like Joe.

The man sitting at the battered gray steel desk looked twenty years older than I remembered him looking yesterday at the hospital. He had his head in his hands and was peering up over his glasses at the door. He let out a sigh when he saw me. I couldn't tell if it was one of resignation or annoyance. Then a second later he inhaled loudly and sat up straight. I thought this was a very strange reaction, until I remembered that Chuck Boyd hadn't clapped eyes on Jessica until now. She was in his direct line of sight through the office door. As usual, she had conquered another of the male species without even trying.

Boyd stood up, shook himself a bit like the shaggy sheepdog he sort of resembled, and came around the desk. "Hi Fiona, I feel so bad. I'm so sorry."

"I know."

His big bear hug left me breathless and feeling a bit weepy. I sucked air, gave myself a mental shake and got down to business. After all, we'd gone through all the condolences at the hospital and I was on a mission to find out why Joe was flying his airplane and not Boyd's yesterday.

I briskly said, "Thanks, Boyd. I'd like you to meet, Jessica. She works in a law firm and is helping me get to the bottom of this all." Now I have no idea what prompted me to say all of this. Maybe I thought the mention of a law firm showed I meant business about getting answers. I was also afraid that sympathy from Joe's friends would bring on the tears again.

He looked a little taken aback by my abruptness. He ignored Jessica's proffered hand and stepped back to let us both squeeze into the little space. There was an awkward silence. We were too close together, practically nose to nose. I straightened my shoulders in a show of determination. Might as well get the burning question over with. "Why was Joe towing your banner with our airplane?"

He let out a big sigh. "I wondered when you'd find that out. Who told you? Peter?"

"Nobody told me. I saw the wreckage myself. Why didn't either of you tell me this before."

"We didn't want to upset you."

"That's the stupidest thing I've ever heard. I'm already upset that Joe's dead and everyone is pointing to me being the cause of it. What would one more thing add to it?"

"What's the significance of not letting Fiona know it was Joe's airplane?" Jessica hadn't said a word up until now and her voice startled Boyd and me out of our eyeball-to-eyeball- staring match.

"Let's sit down and I'll explain." He dusted off one empty chair and moved a pile of grease-stained maintenance manuals off another. He waited until we were both seated, then squeezed past us to sit behind his desk. He leaned back, clasped his hands behind his head, and started.

"Yesterday morning I had a tow job. It was a quickie, three times around the police precinct with a happy birthday banner for our new chief of police. All the local cops chipped in to pay for it. The timing had to be exact because they wanted it to be a surprise during the chief's inspection of the new cruisers that had arrived."

"What's this got to do with Joe?" I know I sounded rude, but I was getting impatient with his rambling narrative.

"I'm getting to it." He sounded a bit testy.

"Let him tell it his way." Jessica seemed to be taking Boyd's side. I sat back in my chair and gave what I hoped was a look saying, *I'm waiting, get on with it.*

"As I was saying, time was of the essence. I set the banner up at dawn and did the pre-flight on my Cub. As I was revving up ready for take-off, I blew a jug and swallowed a valve."

"What?" Jessica beat me to it. I hadn't understood any of the last sentence either.

"Yeah. It was real bad. I was done." Boyd answered.

"The thing about jugs and valves. What do you mean by that?" I thought I knew a bit about airplanes, but this was a new one for me.

Boyd explained, "One of the pistons blew a hole in the cylinder. There was a big bang and lots of smoke. Luckily for me, it happened before I got in the air. I pushed my airplane to the apron and saw that Joe's Super Cub was outside his hangar. I remembered then that he had a banner hook on his airplane. I thought I could talk him into loaning me his airplane for this one quick job." He stopped talking and rubbed his eyes. He looked very sad and tired.

"But you didn't fly it. Joe did." I prompted him to continue.

Boyd sat straighter in his chair. "I looked around for Joe, but he wasn't in his hangar or office. The flight school told me he'd gone for some breakfast. I rushed over to Mama Rosa's and sure enough he was there just about to start his eggs and sausage. At first, he didn't want to loan me the airplane, but when he heard what the job was, he agreed to. It's always good politics to be nice to the new chief of police. Then when we got back to the airfield, he insisted he would fly. He said something about getting some fresh air into his body before wasting the morning with a shrink. I don't know what that meant."

"We had an appointment with a marriage counselor." My words lingered in the space between metal shelves and filing cabinets. I didn't see the point of keeping our marital problems secret anymore. It seemed everyone in town knew about them from what Masters had let out.

Jessica's throat clearing and cough broke the awkward silence. "Do you know why someone would put a plastic bag full of water into Joe's fuel tank?" She voiced the question that had been burning inside me.

"What?" Boyd said, "Where did you hear that?" He sat even straighter in his chair. We now had his full attention.

Jessica told him what Peter had said earlier on. She omitted the part about the police finding a box of baggies in my car. When she was done, he stared at me for the longest time. I gave him my puzzled look, willing him to say something. And he did.

"I thought it was a simple engine failure. And I've been kicking myself because I didn't take the flight. I thought it was that the fates were on my and your side yesterday."

"I don't understand what you mean by the fates being on my side too," I said.

"Joe told me the flight school had a message from you about flying yesterday. He was complaining a bit about it at breakfast. He said you hadn't flown for a long time. He hoped Peter knew that and would be on alert for any stupid mistakes you most likely would make. He was worried you'd do damage to the Cub. I also think he was worried you'd hurt yourself. You would have if you'd been the first to take the airplane up. That's why his Cub was outside and the pre-flight done when mine blew the jug. It was waiting for you."

The concept that I might have died in the crash hadn't occurred to me. For the third time today, bile rose in my throat. I gagged and looked wildly around for something to be sick in. Boyd quickly handed me a well-used, grubby Dunkin' Donuts paper coffee cup but nothing came up. I held it at the ready and took a moment to calm myself, "Who would want to kill me?"

"That's too much of a long shot. You haven't been around for a long time." Boyd's eyes narrowed when he looked at me. I couldn't read what was going on in his mind. Speculation on who killed Joe? Maybe even thoughts on who wanted me gone. I could name a few.

"I'm sure Maria would like to see me dead."

"Why? Joe and you were splitting up. That pleased her. The question most likely is who wanted to get Joe out of the way? Or I could have been the one to get rid of. There was plenty of time between my airplane breaking down and Joe deciding that he would take the flight. Everyone in the flight school knew I wanted to borrow Joe's airplane. Anyone could have put a plastic bag in the tank. It's a two-minute or less job."

"What does the saboteur have to gain by any of your deaths?" Jessica asked. "When we can figure that out, we'll have the killer."

My cell phone buzzed at that moment. It was Peter. "Where are you? I've been looking all over." Peter ignored my icy request to know why it was his business to know where I was and why he was hunting me down. I wasn't in the mood to explain my doings and whereabouts to an ex-policeman who seemed to think I'd put a plastic bag of water into my husband's airplane.

He continued, "I thought you might like to know that the Tomeis are going to the undertakers. You might want to get there ahead of them." He hung up before I could ask the name of the undertaker or the exact appointment time.

Much as I wanted to continue talking over and debating the accident, I wanted more to thwart any funeral plans my in-laws had. I was determined to get there ahead of them. Boyd told me there was only one undertaker in town the Tomeis would use, Burns and Son, and gave us directions. We left via the south side gate and passed a black Crown Victoria on the way out.

"That looks like a police car," Jessica said.

Yes. There's Masters in the passenger seat. Hurry up, I don't want to talk to the cops again today."

Jessica put her foot on the gas as soon as we hit the main road.

RELIEF WASHED over me at the sight of the undertaker's empty parking lot. The Tomeis hadn't yet arrived. Hopefully, they'd follow their usual practice of being late for everything.

The undertaker, or as Burns Junior liked to call himself, the funeral director, wasn't as unctuous as I anticipated. In fact, he was down-to-earth and pleasant. His solicitous remarks hinted that he knew of the Tomeis and my issues. He smiled gravely and ushered us into the two armchairs set before his desk. If the Tomeis showed up, they'd be relegated to the hard, straight-back chairs along the wall. I tried not to feel pleased about that possibility.

"My condolences, Mrs. Tomei. I know this is a trying time for you, especially under these difficult circumstances. Family problems do come to the surface over death. My job is to help you transcend any differences you might encounter and to answer all your questions."

I was comforted but skeptical. I squashed down my two burning questions…the why and who? I knew he wouldn't have an answer for that.

"Our first decision is to find the best way we can to send Joe on his eternal journey." Burns Junior steepled his hands and looked at me.

I hadn't really thought this through. The words 'eternal journey' conjured up visions of Joe doing acrobatic maneuvers in the bright sky without a worry about running out of fuel or stalling in a loop. I stifled a little chuckle; Joe would enjoy that.

"If I cremated him, I could sprinkle his ashes over the airfield."

"We could arrange a ceremony at the airfield if that is what you want. But I don't think the health department will allow you to scatter ashes in a public place."

"I was thinking of throwing them out of an airplane as we fly over the airfield."

"I'm sorry, Mrs. Tomei, but I know that is forbidden."

"Oh, but we did…." I stopped myself just in time. A couple of years ago, we held a lovely ceremony at the airfield for a veteran pilot. His daughter flew his airplane over his house, and sprinkled his ashes over his roof and garden. I remember now hearing mutterings that this was strictly *verboten*. But I was determined to scatter Joe's ashes over his beloved airfield. I know Peter or Boyd would do the honors.

Burns Junior's voice broke into my thoughts. "I believe the family would appreciate a traditional viewing here at our facilities and then a service at church with interment afterward in the family plot. Allow me to show you some options."

He flipped open a portfolio filled with pictures of caskets, flower arrangements, silk linings and pillows. Each photo had a reference number, which I bet correlated to a price list tucked away somewhere in the back where grieving family members can't see. Everything looked luxurious and expensive.

I pointed randomly to the simplest-looking coffin. "How much would this cost?" I was thinking of my very meager personal bank account balance. I bet Joe's account wouldn't have much in it either. All his money was tied up in the airfield. He had to scramble every three months to pull together the property taxes.

"Ah yes, excellent choice Mrs. Tomei. That's our *faux* ebony premiere model with silvered art deco accents. This casket with our buttoned satin interior lining and pleated pillow will make a great presentation." Junior looked discretely at a piece of paper and gave a price that would have made me fall over if I wasn't cocooned deep in the depths of his overstuffed chair.

"Don't you have anything cheaper?" I squeaked. Then regretted my skinflint reaction as Junior frowned and looked down his long nose at me. "This is one of our economy packages, Mrs. Tomei."

I swear, if he uttered that name again, I'd strangle him. I was so sick of being associated with the family. I was beginning to reassess my first impression of liking him.

"Perhaps you would share with us the average cost of a funeral Mr. Burns. You see, we've never had to do this before." Jessica's calm voice cut through the voices in my brain asking how was I going to afford to send Joe off on…what's it called…his eternal voyage? I was hyperventilating at the thought.

Burns Junior's answer didn't help at all. It included embalming, casket and trimmings, flowers, viewing space, services, and internments. "There's no way I can afford that," I whispered to Jessica. Aloud I asked, "So, if I go with no embalming, a closed pine casket, and cremation that will mean no satin pillows and such? How much will that cost?"

That number wasn't much lower and judging by the look on his face, my wishes were not acceptable to Mr. Burns, Jr. Apparently Joe had a lot of friends in town who expected him to be sent off in a traditional catholic way. What was I to do? I didn't think my credit cards would bear the cost.

I was just about to ask about funerals on the installment plan when the office door burst open and, what seemed like, a hoard of Tomeis pushed their way in. The mass of bodies separated out into Mama and Papa Tomei, George and number two son, Anthony. Maria wasn't among them. Maybe the Tomeis told her not to come, even though I'd heard they loved her like a daughter. Or maybe she had the decency stay out of this particular family business. I doubted it, but I was glad not to face her.

"We've come to bury our son." Mama and Papa announced in unison.

The nerve of them. I was the wife, so it was my duty to bury my husband. Incensed by the intrusion, and momentarily forgetting Joe's infidelities and funeral costs, I bristled and got ready to go to war. I wanted to have the privilege of wearing black and walking into the church ahead of everyone. I moved to rise from the chair to face them on an equal footing, when a sharp ankle kick from Jessica stopped me. I sank back into my seat and glared at her. She bent her head and whispered in my ear, "Let it go, Fiona. This is not the fight you want to win."

"Why not?" I hissed back.

Her whispered answer was the dollar figure that Burns had just quoted. She was right. I would take the high road and allow the family take care of things. I took a couple of deep breaths to regain my sanity and equilibrium.

I stood up to greet my in-laws. "Mama Rosa, Papa. I am so sorry for your loss." I wondered if they would return the condolences. I doubted it and I was right. Their only response was to move in closer to the two comfortable chairs. They flanked Jessica and me. It was obvious they expected us to cede our seats. I looked down at Jessica and raised my eyebrows. She nodded, stood up and moved away. I joined her on the hard chairs in the back. The two brothers moved as far away from us as they possibly could.

At that point, we ceased to exist to the people in the room. Burns Junior stood up, shook hands with Papa, George, and Anthony, then gave them manly hugs. He kissed Mama on the cheek and hugged her. I could see where his loyalties lay. He was now officially in the unctuous category.

"We want the best for our son." Mama wiped her eyes with a black lace handkerchief. I wondered if she kept a stack of them for funerals. There were generations of Tomeis in the area.

"We were just going over arrangements, Mama Rosa." Yup, Burns Junior was close to the Tomeis. Only her friends called her that.

"Money is no object, John." Papa leaned forward towards Burns. "We want our son to have a funeral suitable for a successful businessman."

My ears pricked up at this. Joe's name, coupled with being a successful businessman, was an oxymoron in my view. He ran the airfield with his heart, not his head, and it showed in red ink, final demands, and overdraft fees. A movement by George made me look sideways at him. He had shifted abruptly in his seat and started leaning forward to reach over to his father. It looked as if he wanted to get Papa's attention. He caught me looking and sank back with a frown. Something was going on that I didn't know about. I wondered if it was something that he'd taken from the now empty *Real Estate* folder. I toyed with the idea of asking what Papa meant by calling Joe a success then rejected it. Now was not a good time.

"Do you think this is a good plan, Fiona?" Hearing Burns Junior utter my name brought me out of my thoughts. A while ago I'd wished for him to stop calling me Mrs. Tomei, but now I didn't like his use of my first name. It was disrespectful. Yes, there were two Mrs. Tomeis in the room, and he might want to make sure he heard my wishes. But still. I hadn't given him permission to use my given name.

"I'm sorry, I wasn't listening."

"Pay attention, girl." Papa turned around to glare at me.

This put me in pissed-off mode, and it must have shown because Jessica took hold of my hand and gave it a warning squeeze. I sat back and tried to calm myself. I was surprised she hadn't said a word since the Tomei invasion. She answered for me, "I believe those arrangements will meet with Fiona's approval. I assume the cost will be borne by you, sir." She stared straight at Papa.

"Who is this person?" Papa asked as if he hadn't noticed her in this not over-large office.

"This is my friend and advisor, Jessica Feinstein. She is helping me with legal matters." Two could play the game of coolness. I enjoyed the look of consternation on Mama and Papa's faces. I couldn't see George or Anthony's reaction. Jessica graciously inclined her head and gave them the benefit of her smile.

"What do you need an advisor for?" Papa demanded.

"Well, for one thing, I need one here in this room. I am the wife. I get to decide the funeral arrangements." I was ready to go on and on about my rights, when I got another, now harder, hand squeeze from Jessica.

"As I said, Fiona agrees to allow Joe's family to take over all funeral arrangements and expenses. Now, if you'll excuse us, we have an appointment. Please make sure we are informed of all the details." Jessica stood up, and holding firmly to my hand, led me out of the room.

Savoring a momentary victory, I looked back at the open-mouthed quintet and inclined my head in a gracious goodbye.

Outside in the afternoon sun, I turned to Jessica. "Why did you go all formal in there and pull me out? And, what appointment do we have?"

"Don't you get it? They are going to pay for the funeral. Let them take care of everything. You won't win this fight. Let it go. And, as for an appointment, we have one with ourselves. We need to figure out why your husband is perceived to be a brilliant and successful businessman. This description doesn't fit the Joe you talk about. And we have a murderer to find. Let's go home."

"To Manhattan?"

"No, we'll stay at Joe's, I mean your place. The police might not want you to leave the area, even if they haven't said so, and we need to be close to the action." Jessica got into the driver's seat again. "We have to go shopping for food and wine. I'm not eating that family's leftovers anymore, even though they are delicious. Come on, I'm starving. We missed lunch."

CHAPTER 6

"Let's go back to the airfield," I said as Jessica pulled into my driveway.

"Why?" She twisted around to look at me.

"I've got a feeling I missed something in the office. There's got to be something there to make the Tomeis say Joe was a successful businessman."

"If you say so, but first, let's get the groceries inside. Melted chocolate ice cream for dessert is not on my menu plan. And I'm still starving. I'll make sandwiches." Jessica popped the trunk and handed me a couple of grocery bags. "However, the Tomeis probably saw Joe in a different light than you. You told me he was the pampered baby son and that they worshiped him. They might have believed that just because he owned an airfield, he must be rich. That's something I would assume. I mean, airplanes are rich people's toys, aren't they? And Joe has a couple."

"I thought the same way when I first got introduced to the general aviation world. But it isn't completely true. Most of the guys at this small airfield are middle or working-class. They love airplanes and pour all their money into their hobby. Joe can barely pay the bills from the hangar and tie-down fees. His grandfather owned the land

and left it to Joe when he died. I understand the rest of the family was very annoyed about that. Apparently, they wanted to sell the land, but Joe refused to listen to them. Joe inherited his grandfather's love of aviation. George was the only one of his family who ever came out to the airfield. I don't know why. He never went flying. He just hung around."

"Have you looked in the house for any indication of another business?"

"Joe used to keep all his paperwork at the airfield, but I'll take a look around." I shifted the plastic bags around to get a better purchase and moved toward the front door. We'd bought enough food and drink to last a few days. I hoped this meant Jessica was staying on through the weekend. I dumped my bags in the kitchen and left Jessica to put the food away and make sandwiches.

I WAS RIGHT; there were no business papers in the house. There wasn't much space in our tiny ranch to hide anything. Even so, I thoroughly searched the desk, the credenza, and any other cabinet or drawer that I or Joe might have stuffed papers inside. As I searched, I got to thinking about what had changed and what hadn't in the house. The cupboards and drawers were all eerily just as I'd left them. The only papers around were magazines and old newspapers. I forgot what day recycling was, but it was obvious Joe didn't do it often. I started a pile to put out the next garbage day.

What was missing was Joe's laptop. He'd had one when I left. He used it as a backup. I thought back to the airfield office and couldn't remember seeing it there. It was old, so maybe he tossed it. I said as much to Jessica who, had just put the sandwiches on the table.

"Let's eat, then we'll go back to the airfield to see if Joe's laptop is there."

IN LESS THAN ten minutes we were turning up the public access road and driving past the now eerily closed up and silent Mama Rosa's. Friday night was usually their busiest. The long tables filled up quickly with teams of little leaguers coming in for pizza after a long evening on the playing fields. The bar stools and booths got crammed with exhausted New York City commuters filled with TGIF thoughts of cheap wine, pitchers of beer, and plates piled high with pasta and Mama Rosa's famous sauce. I guess they couldn't get the small non-family staff to work both the lunch and dinner shifts today.

The evening sun shone straight down the runway, casting long shadows from parked airplanes lining the taxiway and apron. In the distance, a few airplane watchers lounged in beach chairs under a Cessna wing on the south side. I remember doing that with Joe, Peter, and Boyd. We'd watch the evening parade of jets filled with visitors to New York City descending slowly into Newark Airport's flight pattern. I shook my head to get the bitter-sweet memories out. This wasn't the time to get maudlin.

The fifty-foot corrugated iron hangar door shone strangely gold in the evening light. My key stuck again in the lock. I made mental note to hunt down some graphite. Inside, the cool darkness was a shock from the warmth and light. A faint rustling broke the silence. I hoped it wasn't a mouse. I made yet another mental note to put out some traps, then remembered the cat that used to hang around. Where was Muffy? I hadn't seen him since I left town. Joe used to feed him and he lived somewhere on or near the airfield. Had he died? That would account for the dead animal smell in the office.

We hadn't taken more than a few steps into the hangar towards the office, when a shadow passed by the man door, blocking the last of the sunlight, and a voice called out, "Hey Joe. You there?"

Jessica and I spun around, bumping into each other and knocking over a tin can filled with metal bits. The clatter drowned out the echo of the man's voice.

"Hey man. What did you drop?" The shadow in the door stepped over the sill and moved towards us. It morphed into the shape of a man in a business suit. His eyes obviously hadn't adjusted to the darkness because he kept on talking as if one of us was Joe.

"Ah, there you are." I guess it was Jessica's height and the darkness that deceived him. "I was looking for George, but the restaurant is all closed up. Strange, what's going on?" Without waiting for an answer, the man took another step towards us and before I could speak, he went on, "While I'm here, do you have any questions about the papers I wrote up for you? George told me he gave them you the other day. The deal is kind of time sensitive. I'd be happy to go over the particulars right now if you have time." He finally had to take a breath and I was just about to tell him about Joe, when he got close enough for me to see his features and I assumed he could see us because he said, "Oh, you're not Joe. Is he around?"

Jessica spoke first, "He's not here."

"Who are you?" The man asked.

Jessica chose to ignore the question and asked her standard stalling line. "Can we help you?" She always used it when she didn't want to give out any information. She told me it worked like a charm. People rarely liked asking for help so they blurted out a lot of information. It didn't work this time.

"No. I'll catch up with Joe later." He turned on his heel, walked fast to the man door, and stepped over the threshold.

An unearthly howl shattered the evening.

"Holy shit!" The man leaped back into the hangar and a large orange ball of fur shot through the door.

"What was that?" Jessica had to jump a few feet away from the path of the fur-ball.

"Hey, Muffy. You came back." My eyes followed the orange streak as it whizzed past me into the depths of the hangar.

"Muffy?" Jessica was breathing hard.

"He's the airfield cat. Good, he didn't die. He's supposed to be the mouser, but judging by the smell, he's falling down on the job."

I felt the need to apologize to the man for his scare and moved towards him. "Sorry about the cat."

He was still standing half in and half out of the door and staring at the general direction that Muffy had taken. I got a good look at him. He had sandy hair and the color of skin that the unlucky red-heads have, ruddy even in mid-winter and bright red in the summer. His suit was light gray and had a sheen to it. What is with the suits today? Balasi and the undertaker also wore shiny suits. It is not a look I like. He said nothing, flipped his hand in either a *goodbye* or a *damned cat motion*, and disappeared from sight. I quickly moved to the door in time to see him get into a black Ford Explorer with the words Hasborough Development painted on the door. He gunned the engine and drove off towards the flight school.

"Interesting. I wonder what he develops." Jessica had joined me at the door.

"Why didn't you tell him Joe was dead?" I asked.

"I'm not sure. Maybe it was because he mentioned your brother-in-law and some sort or deal. I hoped he'd say more. I also wasn't in a helpful mood. Why didn't you speak up?"

"I didn't feel like going into explanations about the accident. And, I found it strange he didn't know about it. He can't be from around here. Everybody in town knows everything about everyone. I wonder what he wants. I wonder what kind of business Hasborough Development does."

"We could Google it." Jessica moved towards the office and I followed.

"That reminds me. Look around for Joe's laptop."

It only took a few minutes to check the tiny office space. No laptop. I toyed with the thought of searching the hangar for it, but quickly put off that chore until tomorrow. The lighting wasn't that great in there with the big doors closed. And the shelves were filled to capacity with everything and anything to do with airplanes.

While we waited for the desk top computer to warm up, I wandered around, picking up one thing after another. Joe had touched these things. The more time I spent in his world, the more I missed him. I missed the life we'd had before I caught him and Maria the first time at it, like rutting rabbits, on the old couch in the flight school. Joe said he was drunk and Maria had jumped his bones. It was a one-time fling. Hah! It became a multi-time thing later. My warm thoughts of Joe vanished. *Snap out of it, girl.* I was getting tired of my yo-yo feelings for his memory.

Meow! Muffy had reappeared from wherever his injured dignity has caused him to hide. He bumped his head on my legs and wound between them. He purred like an old engine. He was obviously ravenous. He looked a lot thinner than I remembered and his coat was matted.

"Okay, Muffy. I'll feed you. Let's go and see if there's any food around. Come on old boy."

"Why do you call him Muffy?"

"He looked like a fur muff when he showed up. His coat was long and tangled. We had to shave him. I called him Muffy." I left Jessica to her search and went to make one particular cat happy.

The cat food and bowl were in their usual spot in the hangar. As soon as I put the full bowl on the floor, Muffy dove into it with gusto. I looked at him slurping happily away. He was so much thinner and dirtier than when I left. It wasn't like Joe to neglect him. He let him sit on his lap when he did paper work. Mind you, he often made disparaging remarks about the cat's size and volume of food consumed. I was touched that the cat remembered me, even if it was only as a food dispenser.

"Found it," Jessica called out from the office.

I left Muffy to his meal and went to see. She had thumbed through the business card file while waiting to get on-line and held a card up triumphantly.

"Listen to this…Arnold Watson, President, Hasborough Development Corporation. No address, but a phone number and web site." She typed in the web address and the site popped up. *We Build Your Dream Community.* The headline superimposed an artist's rendering of a dozen McMansions covering acres of impossibly green grass with tastefully situated shrubs and trees. There wasn't much else on the site. The tabs for *About, Projects and Testimonials* opened pages that said; *Under construction please come back later.*

"I bet that empty real estate folder had something to do with this Arnold Watson and his company," I said.

"I wouldn't be surprised. Let's see what else we can find." Jessica, the queen of research, started typing a combination of words. Hasborough figured prominently in Google. She opened a document from the township's zoning commission. Hasborough was seeking a zoning variance for a whole bunch of lot numbers. "Any idea what the airfield lot numbers are?" She asked, "There's no map attached to this document."

"Not off hand. I'll check the property tax file." I flipped through the hanging file folders and came to the familiar tax file. I rifled through the manila folders. "It's empty."

"Maybe he misfiled it."

"I'll look, but I doubt I'll find anything. Joe was meticulous about his filing. Here's the empty folder, but nothing in it. There should be at least two fiscal quarters here. That's two sets of documents gone missing."

"Keep looking while I try the property appraisers' web site." Jessica turned back to the computer. After a few minutes, she threw up her hands in disgust. "I swear the government and education web sites are the worst. There's no good search capability on this one. I put in the airfield address and the Tomei name, and it comes up with an error message. I can't find anything."

"It can wait until tomorrow and the Borough Hall is open." I straightened up from the file drawer.

"Tomorrow is Saturday, they'll be closed."

I'd lost track of the days. It seemed like more than two days since the marriage counselor meeting and the phone call. Exhaustion flooded my brain. I couldn't think any more. Jessica kept on tip-tapping at the keyboard.

"Any luck?" I felt useless standing over Jessica as she scrolled through Google.

"Nothing yet."

"Give it up. Let's go. We'll stop at O'Brady's Inn. Peter and Boyd usually go there. Maybe they know something about this business. It's just down the road." I gathered up my bag and looked around the office for Muffy. I didn't want to lock him in here and I was going to make sure the office was locked up. I was sure he didn't have a secret hole to squeeze in and out of the office. He did have an access hole in the hangar. A groundhog had made it and Joe left it open for him one super cold winter.

Office door safely locked, I looked around the now dark hangar. Muffy was sitting by the man door checking out the exterior world. I checked his food bowl, he'd done a good job of cleaning it out so I topped it up, who knew what time I'd get back here tomorrow. He showed no interest in more food, and stepped over the threshold. We watched him disappear into the twilight, his injured tail twitching over the uncut grass. I double checked the padlock. I didn't want anyone getting in. Of course, if they had keys, this was a moot point. I wished I'd taken the time to get the locks changed for the house and hangar. Another thing to put on my 'to do' list.

Jessica hesitated before turning on the ignition key and turned to look at me. "What are you going to ask Boyd and Peter? They won't know the airfield lot numbers."

"No, but they'll know if Joe was selling the airfield."

"Will they? I wonder. The missing files, the caginess of Arnold Watson and involvement of George all seem a little strange. Didn't you say Boyd wanted to be partners with Joe at one time?"

"Yes, but that means he'd surely know about Watson."

"Not necessarily. Someone wanted Joe dead and to finger you for the murder. I think we should go carefully and not tell everyone our business. We can find out about the lot numbers and such on Monday. There's no rush."

"I feel like there's a rush. So much has happened in two days. I've got lots of questions, but no answers. Let me just ask them if they know anything."

"I guess so, but be careful." Jessica was letting her legal side come out again.

O'Brady's parking lot was surprisingly full. I guess the people who usually went to Mama Rosa's still needed their Friday evening food fix and had opted for the next establishment on the main road. We had to park on the street a block away.

A lone cicada chirped in the bushes hoping for one last love encounter before the chilly evenings arrived. Someone told me once that it would be six weeks from the first cicada chirp to the first frost. I wasn't here for their first chirp. I do miss their evening song now that I live in The City. One day I'll put that bit of folklore to the test. I noticed both Peter and Boyd's vehicles were also on the street, they must have just got there. The early birds all had spaces in the lot.

I hesitated at the door. Was it out of line for a new widow to go into a bar? I probably knew half the people in the place. What had seemed like a good idea at the airfield, now seemed inappropriate. Maybe Jessica was right, I could wait until Monday to find out about Hasborough.

"What's the matter?" Jessica bumped into me from behind.

"I'm not sure this is such a good idea now."

"You're right, let's go." This not wanting to leap into the fray was unlike Jessica.

"But then I'll be thinking about Hasborough all weekend. I've got to go in."

Jessica heaved a sigh, "Then why did you say it wasn't a good idea?"

"Because it doesn't look good for a new widow to go into a bar."

"Oh please! Who cares about what people think? But, if you don't want to go in, I can go by myself. I know what the guys look like."

I thought about this for a moment and it was tempting. "Would you? I just feel that everyone will think I'm a bad person for going in there."

"That's ridiculous. You were getting a divorce and you said the whole town knew about you and Joe. They are all probably talking about you right now if the Tomeis have anything to do with it. Why not hold your head up high and ignore them all? Come on. I'll hold your hand if you want." She laughed and held her hand out.

She was right. What did I care what people thought about me? I took her up on her offer and, hand in hand, we marched into O'Brady's.

The place had been one of my favorites. The oval bar of dark wood smack in the center of the room was a great place to see and be seen. Because the television screens were around the perimeter of the room, the people at the bar had to talk to each other. If you wanted to watch TV, you had to swivel around in your seat to stare at the nearest one, or squint at the set across the bar on the other side of the room. O'Brady's was a very social bar. And the food was quite good. You could eat at the bar, or one of the twenty or so tables dotted around the one room.

This evening, the place didn't feel very social. As we stepped into the room, dozens of pairs of eyes checked us out. The noise level dropped quite a bit on our entrance. I recognized many of the people there. I scanned the place, Peter and Boyd were in their usual spots on the narrow curve of the bar. They too had turned to check us out and both their mouths were open. I had the full attention of everyone in the place. I suddenly felt very powerful. I tilted my chin up, squeezed Jessica's hand once, let it go, and walked alone towards Peter and Boyd. It was a pretty amazing trip. As I passed each table, the person sitting nearest to me reached out a hand to touch mine and muttered, "Condolences." I graciously inclined my head left and right and thanked each person. It seemed I didn't have a town full of enemies after all. When we got to the bar, the two men sitting next to Boyd scrambled to their feet and indicated we should sit on their stools. I shook my head, "No thanks, we're not staying."

"Do you want a drink?" Boyd asked.

I did, desperately, but didn't think it was the right thing to do. "Not now, thanks."

Peter got up from his stool and came to stand beside Boyd. "If you're not staying and you don't want a drink, what happened to bring you both in here?"

"What is this business with Hasborough Development?" I asked.

Peter and Boyd looked at each other, then Boyd sucked in air and asked, "How'd you hear about them?"

"A guy from the company stopped by the hangar. He seemed to be on good terms with Joe. He left before we could tell him about Joe's unfortunate accident."

"That would be Arnold Watson," Peter found his voice.

"He's George's friend. Not Joe's," Boyd added.

"He started nosing around a few weeks ago. He's nothing to worry about. Forget about it." Peter returned to his bar stool.

"He mentioned some papers he'd given Joe." Jessica stared at each of them, compelling and answer.

Peter and Boyd exchanged more glances. I thought there was a question in their look. Peter shrugged his shoulders and said, "We might as well tell her. She'll find out soon enough."

"Find out what?" I didn't like the idea that Joe's friends and I thought mine, were keeping things from me.

"Joe was pissed at his brother over something. I don't know what as he didn't share this time." Peter gulped his beer.

"He was always annoyed at George. And George with him. What is new with that?" I asked, remembering the constant arguments over the airfield and the restaurant.

"It was far more hostile this time," Boyd answered. "It was getting so bad I didn't like to eat at Mama Rosa's in case George spat into my food. He knew I wanted to put money into the airfield and be Joe's partner and for some reason, he didn't like that."

"Yeah. Joe came to blows with George a few days ago. They stopped as soon as I showed up, but it was pretty nasty." Peter downed the last of his beer and slid off his bar stool. "Excuse me a moment. Got to get rid of some beer." A few of the diners spoke to him as he navigated his way to the men's room. I couldn't tell if he answered. I wondered what they said. Probably something about the accident. Peter was a well-known authority in town on things related to police and airfield news.

"So that's it? That's all you didn't want to share with me? That's lame."

Boyd's eyes slid away from my stare. "I've never seen Joe come that close to hitting George before. And then the accident. Thought you'd be upset."

"Does Detective Masters know about the fight?" Jessica asked.

"I guess so. The whole town was talking about it the next day. You sure you two don't want a drink?" Boyd looked at his now empty glass. I knew the protocol. A man can't order a refill without offering to buy drinks for the new arrivals.

"Thanks, but no." I had had enough of all this and it didn't look like Peter was coming back soon from the men's room or that Boyd wanted to talk anymore. "Come on Jessica."

Jessica nodded and started to turn, then stopped. "By the way Boyd, have you any idea where Joe might have put his laptop?"

"Sure I do. It's in my hangar. He asked me to scrub it. Seems he's bought a new one."

"There's no new one around," I said.

"Have you done the erasing yet?" Jessica asked.

"No. He left it with me the night before his accident. I haven't had time. I'll get to it."

"Don't do that," Jessica and I said this at exactly the same time.

Boyd stared first at me, then at Jessica. "Why? What's up?"

"We're looking for something, anything that'll shed light on Joe's business dealings. There's nothing on his office desktop."

"He didn't like to keep much on that. Too many people had access to the place."

"Like who?" I asked.

"He didn't lock up during the day. So pretty much anybody on the airfield."

I couldn't think of anything more to ask and the subdued atmosphere in the room was getting awkward. People were still casting glances at us and speaking in hushed tones. "I'll come by tomorrow and get the laptop."

"We should leave and let all these people enjoy their meal. And we need to eat." Jessica took my arm.

"Yes, food will be good. Let's go. I'm starving. Say goodbye to Peter for us."

"Bye, Boyd." Jessica led the way to the door. This time nobody interrupted our passage with messages of sorrow.

It was now fully dark outside. The stars twinkled among the lights of the Newark-bound airplanes. I took a deep breath of cool night air to clear my mind.

"There's something more those guys aren't sharing," Jessica spoke the thoughts I was thinking.

CHAPTER 7

Jessica volunteered to fix dinner, muttering about having too many carbs last night. She swore she was getting fat. My statement that one pasta meal won't make anyone fat and that I'd seen a good lasagna dish in the freezer, got me a dirty look and a reminder of all the healthy food we'd just bought. Jessica had fallen off her low-carb wagon and wasn't having anything to do with the forbidden food for now. She informed me that cooking helped her think. I left her to it and wandered out of the kitchen area.

I was tired, but too restless to sit quietly watching TV. Now I wished I'd asked Boyd to bring Joe's laptop to the house tonight. At least I could then surf the net. There wasn't much to read around the house except the old newspapers and magazines cluttering up the place. I could sort and bundle some of the stacks of papers and get them ready for recycling day. I put a CD in the player and sweet vibes of The Modern Jazz Quartet filled the room. Jessica was making soft cooking noises and a delicious aroma had started to seep out of the kitchen. It was all very peaceful and cozy. I flipped through the local news sections just to see if there were any tidbits about people I knew. The tension of the last two days slowly drained out of me as my eyes scanned small-town news stories about births, weddings, anniversaries, and triumphs on the high-school playing fields. I drifted off into the land of good old memories and slowly turned the pages. Then I saw it. I sat bolt upright and focused on a recently seen face superimposed on a very familiar aerial photo of the airfield.

"Jessica, look at this." I scrambled to my feet and fell over the ottoman in my haste to get to the kitchen. I picked myself up and then collided with Jessica coming to see what I was excited about. We disentangled ourselves and I smoothed out the now crumpled paper. "It's that Arnold Watson guy." Together, we read the month-old article.

Developer Unveils Ambitious Plans for New Subdivision

New neighbors will bring economic prosperity to the township if Hasborough Development Corporation follows through on its promise to build one thousand new homes and a retail center with a town square on the three hundred undeveloped acres on the southwest side of the township.

"The airfield isn't undeveloped. Even the grassed-over area in the back is used for ultra-lights, the banner tow operation, and the model airplane guys. This is so wrong." I pointed at the newspaper.

"I bet this was what the Real Estate file contained," Jessica said.

"But why was it empty? What else does this article say?" We read on and again the reporter got the facts wrong. It stated that the airfield was inactive. This was so not true. One hundred and thirty or so airplanes call the place home. There were twenty occupied hangars and three businesses on the airfield. The owner was named as George Tomei. Another wrong fact that I vehemently pointed out to Jessica.

"Could George have bought it off Joe?" she asked.

"Never in a million years. I know I've been away from Joe for some months, but he couldn't have changed that much. The airfield was his life. Even if by some remote chance he needed to sell, it wouldn't be to George. They didn't get on that well. George wanted Joe to cook at the restaurant. Joe hated cooking and anything to do with restaurants and catering. Besides, George doesn't have that kind of money."

"You said that Joe had problems meeting the quarterly tax payments. Maybe George bought the tax liens."

"What's that?"

"After a certain time of not paying taxes, municipalities put a lien on the property and then every so often they sell those liens to investors who can then foreclose on the property if the owner doesn't pay them back the monies they laid out for the taxes."

"That's a dirty thing to do. How long does it take for liens to come to auction?"

"Months. Sometimes years. It depends on the municipality. And they don't come cheap. The purchaser has to pay off all the taxes."

"I'll call Joe's lawyer. He'll know about this deal. He did the business stuff as well as the divorce." I hunted through an old phone directory and found the number then, forgetting how late it was, I dialed. All I got was his office voicemail system. I left a message for him to call me. "I wonder if Joe has his cell number." Then I remembered that all of Joe's effects were still with the police, including his cell phone. I should get it back. I added it to my mental to-do list for tomorrow. I slumped into the chair feeling a bit defeated.

"Dinner is nearly ready. Open some wine and I'll finish it up." Jessica squeezed my shoulder and disappeared into the kitchen. She was a true friend, even if the coming meal probably wouldn't have any stomach-satisfying carbs.

THE CLAMORING of the telephone broke through the television noise. I stirred a little but was loathe to answer it and tear myself away from a re-run episode of *Castle*. I hadn't seen this one and we were just getting to an interesting part where Beckett and Castle might kiss for the first time. They'd been dancing around their mutual attraction for far too long. I wasn't sure I wanted them to consummate the relationship or not. But I sure wanted to find out. Jessica didn't move from her curled-up corner of the couch.

"I suppose I'd better get that." I heaved myself off the saggy, but comfortable cushions, and headed over to the faux rotary phone by the front door. The journey took me too long to catch the caller and the answering machine clicked on.

"Hey Joe, I got a call on my office phone from your wife. What's all that about? Call me on my cell. I'm in Atlantic City with a client." It was Bill Dewey, Joe's lawyer.

I lunged for the phone too late, he'd hung up.

So, Dewey didn't know about the accident. I was very surprised. To tell the truth, it had crossed my mind how odd it was that he hadn't made an appearance at either the hospital, the house, or the funeral home. He was a good friend of Joe's and was once my friend too. I didn't relish the thought that I now had to tell him Joe was dead and that he should be here in town dealing with Joe's will and family. Should I call him back? It was late and I didn't want to get into the sadness of passing on bad news. We'd had a great dinner of salmon, asparagus, and wild rice with mushrooms, finished off with a rich Belgium chocolate ice cream. Thanks to Jessica's culinary efforts, I felt mellow and relaxed. We'd limited ourselves to only one bottle of wine between the two of us and we'd spread out the drinking over the meal and the rest of the evening. I decided to call. He had after all told Joe to call him back.

I picked up the phone, before registering that this old receiver and answering machine didn't have the last number called feature of newer phones. "Jessica, can you remember that number to dial to hear who called you last?"

"Let me think. It was star something or other. I used it a few times back in the days when those heavy-breathing perverts called in the middle of the night."

"You're sounding like an old lady with your *back in the days*." I giggled. Maybe half a bottle of wine had been too much.

"Star sixty-nine. That's it. And I'm not old. I wonder what happened to the perverts. How do they get their sick thrills now we have caller ID?"

"They stalk online now." I punched in star sixty-nine and was pleased to hear the disembodied voice intone, "The last number called was ……"

My heart beat faster as I dialed Dewey's number. What was I going to say? When I called Jessica two days ago, I started crying as soon as I said the words, "Joe is dead." They were so final. The same thing happened to me when I had to tell my aunt that her sister, my mother, had died. Even though we knew it was inevitable. I held my breath as the phone rang on the other end. Half of me hoped Dewey wouldn't pick up and I'd get a chance to leave a voice message.

But no such luck, he picked up. "Hey Joe, what's up?"

"It's Fiona. Joe's dead." My words came out abrupt and harsh, but it was all I could manage. My eyes started to fill up. The silence at the other end of the phone dragged on for too long. "Dewey, are you there?"

"I'm here, Fiona. What happened? Why didn't anyone tell me? I can't believe it."

"He was in an airplane crash. I think you should come back here. There's stuff going on. I need you."

"Fiona, I'm not your lawyer now. I'm Joe's."

"Yes, but with him dead, there is no divorce. Please, Bill." It just occurred to me that I desperately needed to see his kind, wrinkled, chubby face and that angelic halo of white hair. Bill Dewey was like everybody's favorite uncle. I was devastated when Joe named him as his divorce lawyer. I wanted him. But in my heart of hearts, I knew he'd represent Joe. He'd been at his christening. And he sided with Joe when the Tomei clan got on his case about time spent at the airfield.

"I can't tonight. I've had a couple of drinks too many to make the two-hour drive right now. I'll get on the road first thing in the morning. Tell me what happened."

It took me a long time to go over the accident and the police investigation. I had to keep stopping to blow my nose. When I was done, he said, "I'll see you in the morning. Come to my office around ten. Goodnight." I noticed he didn't say, 'Don't worry.' Or offer his condolences. It didn't matter, I could feel the tension leaving my body at the thought of Bill Dewey being on my side.

"Did you ask him about the development plans for the airfield?" I hadn't realized that Jessica had cleaned up the remnants of dinner while I was on the phone and hadn't heard my end of the conversation.

"No, I only told him about the accident and the police. We're seeing him tomorrow." I went on to tell Jessica what a wonderful, teddy bear of a man Dewey was. She looked a bit skeptical and muttered something about the den of thieves in this town and how I was sure he wasn't one of them. I let it pass. I was tired and I'd missed seeing if Castle and Beckett kissed. I'd catch that episode another day. It was bedtime. There was a lot to do tomorrow. I hadn't bought any clothes, nor got the locks changed. My last thought before falling asleep was that I had to start writing a list of to-dos.' I had far too many to keep in my head.

CHAPTER 8

The whirring of the tiny propeller on the miniature aircraft made out of beer cans on top of Bill Dewey's mailbox brought Jessica to a full stop. She stared at it, shook her head and rolled her eyes. "Is everyone in this town airplane-crazed?"

"Not everyone," said Fiona. "With the exception of Joe, the current Tomeis hate everything to do with airplanes and the airfield. It might be something to do with Joe's grandfather. He learned to fly during the war and bought the airfield when he got out. Apparently, his wife and her family were against it and there were some bitter arguments. He left it all to Joe and nothing to anybody else. The original townspeople tolerate the airfield, some even love it. It was here before the town existed and drove the economy in the area for a while. The history buffs tell stories of a flying circus, stunt airplanes and a carnival. The first houses built belonged to the people working at the airfield. I understand it was a stop on the new air postal route. Horses raced the mail to the train station a mile away and then the letters got to New York City by fast train in less than two hours. It was a miracle in modern postal service. Now the newcomers, they're a different story."

"How so?" Jessica asked.

"They hate it. They say the noise of the airplanes disturbs their lives. Some are scared one will drop out of the sky onto their house."

"I'd be scared of that. But surely they knew about the airplanes when they moved?"

"The newcomers bought in the housing development at the end of the runway. They must have heard the airplanes when they were looking to buy. But no, they denied all knowledge of the airfield. Said they were lied to by the developer and tried to sue. When that failed, they tried to get the airfield closed. They are active in the local council meetings. It is an ongoing battle with them and land-hungry housing developers." I was getting steamed up by now, remembering the argument that had been going on for years. The housing boom had spawned thousands of new homes in the area, mostly McMansions built on farmland. Some were nestled against the airfield's western perimeter, under the flight path. At every town meeting, there'd be some newbie complaining about the airfield and demanding it be shut down. "Since I moved here, three cars have run off the road into people's living rooms, but no airplane crashes — until Joe's." I shook my head to get the visual of the mangled Super Cub out of my mind.

"And you say the old residents don't mind the place?"

"Like I said, the airfield was here first, and even though generations have come and gone, they're all used to it. Many walk their dogs there. We get joggers on the taxiways and the kids learn to ride their bikes on the stretch between the hangars on the south side."

"What about security? I notice there's only a fence around part of it."

"That fence was put up by the state after 9/11 in an attempt to placate the fearmongers. But the money ran out before completion. Joe got some heat from the town council about finishing it, but he ignored them. It was a state or federal problem, not his." We reached Bill Dewey's office door.

I knocked sharply and opened it to his shouted, "Enter." He met us halfway across the room and grabbed me in a huge bear hug.

"Oh, Fiona honey, I'm so sorry." My tears started up at the sorrow in his voice. I hugged him tightly back and when I'd disentangled myself, I saw tears in his eyes. Here was someone in town who was on my side.

"Thanks, Bill. This is my friend Jessica Feinstein." I pointed to her.

Dewey glanced over to where she stood near the door and gave a little wave-like salute, then turned to me. "Good, you've got a friend with you. Is she staying over?"

"I don't know for how long. She has to get back to work sometime."

"I hope you can stay, Jessica. I think Fiona is going to need all the support she can get."

I didn't like the sound of that. "What do you mean, all the support I can get?" I asked.

"Of course, I'll stay. For as long as Fiona needs me," Jessica answered.

"Good. Why don't we all sit down?" Dewey moved a stack of papers off two of the chairs and placed them on the already over-flowing credenza. "Coffee, anyone?" He started pouring from a small coffee maker perched on a cardboard document box without waiting for our answers.

I looked over to Jessica, raised my eyebrows and she nodded. Dewey handed us mugs of steaming hot, pungent liquid. I took a sip and gagged. I'd forgotten his penchant for teeth rotting, strong, black-as-coal-tar, caffeine. "Can I get some sugar?"

"Me too," Jessica added. This was a first. She never touches the stuff. This coffee was over the top strong even by her standards. Dewey took back our mugs, spooned out an unknown quantity of sugar, stirred the black liquid with a pencil, and handed them back. Jessica's and my eyes locked. I shrugged and took a sip. She followed suit. The drink was oversweet, but more palatable than before. It defi-nitely wasn't the designer coffee I'd gotten used to in Manhattan.

Dewey settled down behind his desk. "I've been on the phone with Detective John Masters. He owes me a few favors and thinks I'm only Joe's lawyer, not yours."

"Well, you're not really my lawyer, though I wish you were. I was upset when Joe got to you before I could ask."

"You know I had to represent Joe, since he's my godson. Anyhow, I'm yours now. I also had a talk with that young lad who was representing you in the divorce. I told him the divorce was off and that I'd be handling the estate now. He'll be sending you a bill for past work. But you're all mine now. Agreed?" Dewey looked at me fiercely, daring me to disagree.

"Yes." I smiled at the thought of Mortimer Weiss being called a young lad. He was in his forties and battling with gray hair. I think he had an investment in men's hair dye, the amount he used. I had a mental picture of his Armani-clad chest puffing up in indignation. He was the youngest partner in the firm, but his seniors were all in their sixties. And he took pains to point out that he was in line for a promotion. I looked sideways at Jessica and could see the smile lurking behind her hand. I would bet on her making sure Mort knew he had been called a 'young lad' when she got back to the office.

"What did Masters have to say?" Jessica asked.

"He had a mechanic friend from Princeton look at Joe's airplane. The guy found some remnants of a plastic bag in the fuel tank."

"We know that." Jessica interrupted Dewey. He frowned at this. I knew he wasn't used to people breaking into his lectures. She flashed him a smile and he visibly melted. Another strike for beauty. I wish I had her assets.

"The plastic was sent to police forensics along with a box of baggies found in your car Fiona." Dewey continued. "The Tomeis know about this and I guess they told Maria Avernus, because she is raising holy hell and accusing you of a lot of nasty stuff, including causing the crash."

"What grounds does she have?"

"She's saying that you aren't happy with the divorce settlement and want all of the airfield and the house."

"That's ridiculous. I couldn't have done it."

Dewey shifted in his chair and looked uncomfortable. My first thought was his arthritis was acting up until he said, "That's not what they are saying. Apparently, you were at the airfield the morning of the crash. So, in their eyes, you did have opportunity."

This was a nightmare. I thought Dewey was on my side and now he was saying I had the opportunity. I looked over at Jessica. Was she on my side? She gave me a small smile. I couldn't read the sentiment behind it.

"Enough said about what people are saying. Let's ask ourselves some questions, which are…" Dewey leaned back in his chair and started ticking them off. "Was Joe's death a mechanical accident, pilot error, or murder? If the latter, who did it and why? The motive is the key here."

Hearing the words murder and motive from Dewey kind of shocked me. I don't know why. Detective Masters had hinted at it. Jessica and I had danced around the subject a few times. I'd even thought of it. The Tomeis and Maria were broadcasting it all over. But to hear the word murder said out loud was shocking. I guess I'd been flying on autopilot for the past two days. Half wondering who and why, but also immersed in surprising to me, grief and loss.

"Who benefits from Joe's death?" I might as well be the one to say it aloud. It was like an elephant in the room. I knew of one person—me. But I hoped Dewey and Jessica would come up with a second or third. They didn't answer and the silence stretched out.

Dewey finally spoke up, "Joe didn't change his will when you started divorce proceedings, Fiona. He hoped you'd change your mind after a few sessions with the marriage counselor. When we talked last week, he said he'd reformed and wanted to get his marriage back."

I raised my eyebrows at this. Not much reformation had taken place if those black lace, crotchless panties, and peek-a-boo bra were anything to go by. I decided not to say this out loud. I wanted Dewey on my side and if he thought Joe was still seeing Maria, he might change his mind. I had to remember that Dewey's loyalties were first and foremost to Joe and his memory.

"What does his will say?" Jessica interrupted my thoughts.

"Everything goes to Fiona."

"So, she's the one with the big motive." Jessica did more than acknowledge the elephant in the room. She went over and patted it. And I thought she was my friend. I glared at her. She reached over to squeeze my hand. "Don't worry, sweetie. I know you couldn't kill anyone. You're too gentle."

This mollified me a little, but I was still worried. "Where does all of this put me? Is Detective Masters going to arrest me? I didn't kill Joe, but everyone seems to think I did."

"Not everyone, Fiona, just the Tomeis and Maria. Masters is a fair man. He'll examine all the evidence. Everything is circumstantial at the moment. Masters won't do anything until the NTSB or FAA have finished with their investigation, and they haven't even started it."

"If Fiona inherits everything, how long will it take before she gets control of the airfield?" Jessica asked.

"Probate could take some time. Then there's the key person insurance."

"What is that?" I didn't even know Joe had insurance let alone this kind.

"If the key person in a business is incapacitated, the insurance covers loss of earnings that person would bring in," Jessica answered before Dewey could.

"Joe didn't earn much."

"It was written when his grandfather was alive. He named Joe as the key person. Joe kept the premiums going. He felt it was like his workman's comp," Dewey explained.

"Who gets the money?"

"Whoever gets the airfield. And, at the moment, that's you, Fiona."

"How much is it?" I hardly dared ask, but I really wanted to know. I know I sounded very mercenary.

Dewey's answer made me gasp, "One million! I can save the airfield."

"Don't get all excited. They won't pay out immediately. Insurance companies don't like giving money when there is suspicion of foul play."

We were back to me being a suspect again. I felt sick. A hundred thoughts and questions raced inside my head. They came fast and I couldn't isolate one to make sense of anything. Then one thought popped out. "I've had two strange visitors these last two days. What do you know about…?" In my stress, their names flew out of my head.

"Demetri Balasi and Arnold Watson." Jessica came to my rescue.

"Yes, those guys. They both seem to have some sort of business agreement with Joe. Balasi came to the house. And Watson was at the airfield." I looked at Dewey to see if he reacted to the names.

Dewey shifted again and his chair squeaked in protest. He didn't speak for what seemed to me to be too long a pause. Then with a sigh he started, "I don't recall Arnold Watson. But I do know Demetri Balasi. He's Maria's cousin and, I believe, big trouble. Stay away from him. I can't imagine Joe had anything to do with him. As to this Watson guy, I don't know of any business dealings Joe has apart from the Federal Aviation Authority."

The FAA business was news to me. Joe was passionate about being an independent operator. He kept his dealings with the FAA to the bare minimum for compliance's sake.

Dewey must have seen the astonishment on my face because he elaborated, "Joe was hurting for money, and your divorce threatened to bankrupt him. The three Cessnas he leased to the flight school are getting old and need new engines and a few other expensive parts. Existing hangar and tie-down rents aren't enough to pay airfield maintenance and taxes. The township slapped a lien on the place last quarter to get his taxes. He doesn't, sorry…didn't, have much time to pay up and lift the lien. He had to raise some money before the township sold his liens. A contact I have said someone was asking about buying them up before the grace period. Poor Joe was surrounded by problems." From the look Dewey gave me, I knew he counted me as one of the problems. He continued, "The newcomers to this town have started pushing again to close the airfield. Joe figured out that if he could sell the development rights to the FAA, they would grant him funding to fix the runway, taxiways, apron, and hangars. You know how derelict everything is. A revamped airfield would attract more airplanes with tie-down and hangar fees. This is the closest airfield to New York City. He was also talking to the state police to base their helicopters here."

Now it was my turn to squirm in my chair. An unreasonable sense of guilt took over. Was I really responsible for all of Joe's worries and woes? I opened my mouth to defend myself, but Jessica cut in first.

"According to the newspaper, Arnold Watson seems to think he's getting the development rights. He wants to build houses on the airfield."

"Oh yes, that bunch of crap. Now I remember Watson. He's Hasborough Development. When Joe saw that article in the paper, he went ballistic. Lucky for all, Watson was out of town when the news broke. We believe one of the newcomers had the story put in the paper in the hope it'd push Joe to sell."

"Do you have the lot numbers for the airfield?" Jessica asked.

"Why do you want them?" I sensed puzzlement in Dewey's voice.

"We saw a zoning variance request online to change industrial to housing and wondered what lots they were. There were enough lot numbers to make us think it was the airfield. It was dated a few weeks ago," I answered.

"Most likely they're the airfield lot numbers. Hasborough is being pushy about building around here. I don't know them off the top of my head, but I'll check my files." Dewey looked around his office. I didn't hold out much hope for him being able to retrieve the information quickly. It looked like his filing system favored the teetering pile method, with the newest on top. There wasn't much in the way of clear space around. He picked up a couple of sheets of paper, looked at them and put them back. "I'll get to it later. Not sure where I put it. Doesn't Joe have a tax file? The lot numbers will be in there."

"We couldn't find it," Jessica said.

"That's strange. Joe's not like me. He has a filing system. He's neat." Dewey laughed ruefully, looking around his own personal disaster zone. "If it's urgent, I'll start hunting now." He heaved himself out of his chair and lumbered over to a pile of papers on the third chair.

"Never mind, we can get the numbers from the tax office later." If Bill Dewey started moving papers, I feared we'd get roped into sorting and filing, and I didn't have time for that. I wanted to concentrate on Joe's finances. I hadn't wanted Joe to bankrupt himself over our divorce. It was news to me that he felt I was pushing to get money from him. I needed to have a discussion with Mortimer Weiss when I got back into the City. I should have taken more control over the divorce proceedings. All I wanted was my dignity back and I thought that by divorcing I could start my life over with a clean slate. I didn't want Joe's inheritance. His grandfather had left him the house and the airfield before I met him. I didn't want an airfield or even half of one. I just wanted half our savings. But it sounded as if there wasn't any of that left now.

"Tell me more about the business dealings with the FAA." This wasn't really pertinent to my problems with the accusations flying around, but I wanted to know.

"There was a meeting scheduled for last week, but it got canceled because of the government shut-down, the sequestering."

"Who else knows about this?" Jessica asked.

"Just about everybody. There's no reason to keep it a secret. The township is about equally divided over this. Some think a vibrant airfield will bring money to the town. But many are against it because someone is spreading rumors that corporate jets will be screaming in here."

"Well, could they?" Jessica asked.

Dewey snorted with laughter. "No way. The runway isn't long enough. And there's no land to make it longer. I overheard one guy at the supermarket say the Concorde was coming in and all their houses would get flattened by the sonic boom. I straightened him out. He didn't even know that the Concorde hadn't flown since 2003 and it would have needed a runway that took over the whole town." Dewey shook his head and laughed.

Jessica nodded. I wondered how much she understood about all the aviation talk. She seemed to be cottoning on quickly. I hadn't realized how much a part of my life airplanes and the people who loved them were. I would fill her in later about Bill Dewey being the oldest pilot on this airfield. He dated back to Grandpop Tomei's time. Rumor has it that Dewey was Grandpop's first student. His passion for the airfield matched Joe's.

"What happens now to the airfield? There is no owner. Fiona has no money and the life insurance people won't pay until the crash is investigated." Jessica beat me to the question now foremost in my mind. Yes, she was looking out for me.

"I am Joe's executor and will take over the business dealings." Dewey got up to get more coffee. We both shook our heads when he offered us a refill.

"So, if Watson and Balasi approach Fiona, we can refer them to you?" Jessica said.

"By all means. It'll be a pleasure to deal with them." Dewey chuckled and took a sip of his coffee. By the grimace, I guess it hadn't improved by sitting on the hot plate for half an hour or more. It might be undrinkable even by Dewey's low standards.

"When you say, a pleasure, do you mean you'll entertain their proposals?"

I could tell by Jessica's slipping into her formal tone, that she wasn't happy with what Dewey was saying. I wondered why.

I guess Dewey noticed the change in her tone because he shot her a strange look and answered, "I'll listen. We need to know what's going on."

Jessica sat up straighter and took a breath. This was one of her tells. She was going to argue with Dewey. I needed to cut off this line of conversation. I didn't want to antagonize Dewey.

"We've taken up too much time here. I've got things to do like feed Muffy. Thanks, Bill. Just don't sell my airfield out from under me." My words surprised me. Up until now, I'd only thought of the place as Joe's airfield. Now I realized I really wanted to keep it and run it. I missed the aviation life.

"Don't worry, Fiona. I won't do anything that Joe didn't want done. And, I'm glad Muffy is back. Joe was worried about him. Told me he'd disappeared about a week or more ago."

"Yes, he's back. Looking a little thin." I touched Jessica's arm and jerked my head towards the door. "Bye Bill. Thanks for everything." I waved goodbye and walked out.

Once we'd got out of earshot, I turned to Jessica. "What happened in there? Why did you get nasty?"

"I wasn't nasty. I was very polite."

"I know you were polite, but you were nasty polite. Why?"

"You know me. I'm a suspicious New York City girl. I need to be won over and I'm not convinced Dewey has your best interests at heart. You said he was Joe's godfather and friend of his grandfather. That puts him on the Tomei friend list. Someone is going to a lot of trouble to make the town and police think you put water in Joe's fuel tank. You're the only one who benefits from his death. Dewey was very clear about that. There has to be a reason why someone wanted Joe dead. I know it isn't you. But I'm not sure about anyone else. Peter and Boyd say they are on your side. But remember, first and foremost they are Joe's friends and you are, in a sense, Joe's antagonist. I heard Dewey say that Joe was reformed. But the evidence of the black underwear belies that. He was sleeping with someone recently. I don't trust anyone in this town. I guess I'm paranoid, but the less we tell people, the better off we'll be. We've got to figure this out ourselves. The will and insurance policy can be used against you."

I was touched by Jessica's loyalty. But I wasn't sure I agreed with her. If I couldn't trust Dewey, Boyd, or Peter, who could I turn to? I handed the car keys to Jessica. "You drive. I need to think." My head ached. I felt very alone. "Thanks for being here with me." I gave Jessica a hug.

"Where to?" She squeezed me tight and got into the car.

"Some decent coffee first, then the airfield and Muffy. Turn left, there's a gourmet coffee shop in the shopping mall on the other end of town. That stuff that Dewey brewed is rotting my teeth."

I thought about what Jessica said. People were pointing fingers at me, the outsider. Everyone we'd talked to so far knew Joe from a long time before I met him. Well, maybe not Balasi and Watson, but everyone else, even the police. The solution rested in what Joe was thinking and doing over the past few months. I said as much to Jessica.

CHAPTER 9

The airfield was again quieter than it should be on a nice day. We came in from the south side entrance to get Joe's laptop from Boyd. But his hangar was closed and a note on the door read, 'Gone Flying.' It figured. Saturday was a big banner towing day.

Jessica remembered to check for aircraft before crossing the runway to the north side. The flight school was open and I saw people moving around inside when we drove past, but their airplanes were all at their tie-downs. I guess, as the possible new airfield owner, I should be worried that nobody was renting or taking flying lessons. If the flight school went out of business, the airfield would suffer from the rental loss. I was torn, I wanted to get my head around the thing I know best, finances. But I knew I should focus on other matters. Things like how was I to get out from under the town-wide cloud of suspicion. And the reason for Joe's death. I couldn't wait for Washington to decide to get back to work and the FAA to come out to investigate. I needed answers now so the insurance people would free up the key-man money. Joe used to tease me about my impatience. He'd say that I'd be early for my own funeral. And now here I was planning his funeral. Well technically the Tomeis were planning it. I made a mental note to call up the undertaker and see what had been decided. All of these thoughts couldn't keep me from feeling a bit happy about the day. The sun was brilliant. White clouds dotted the sky like little powder puffs. The last of the summer birds darted around, sucking up insects and nectar from the remaining goldenrod. This airfield was a little bit of paradise in a crowded urban landscape.

Muffy was waiting outside the hangar. He rushed over to us, tail straight up in the air with no evidence of Arnold Watson's assault on it. He threaded himself in and out of my legs, meowing loudly with his tail now at full twitch mode. I made it to the man door without falling flat on my face and opened up. It was good that the place was still locked up. Hopefully, no visitors were lurking inside. I still didn't know how many keys were in the hands of Joe's friends and family. I made yet another mental note to get the locks here and at the house changed. I should have done it the day after George barged in. And, horrible thought, what if Maria has one? I now had a lot of mental notes bouncing around in my brain.

Muffy jumped over the threshold and rushed to his still full food bowl. He must have been hungry as the food was congealed and disgusting looking. Any self-respecting cat would have shunned it.

"Hey Muffy. Why didn't you use your secret hole to get in?" I scratched his bony back as he gobbled up the remains of yesterday's meal.

"What's this secret hole you're talking about?" Jessica looked around the dim hangar.

"There's a place where he can get in. I've never seen it, but I know Muffy comes in and out of the hangar when the big doors are closed. I can't believe Joe would close it up, he liked the cat. This is an outside wall, so it must be somewhere." I looked around. To my left were metal shelves filled with aircraft parts. Tool boxes and tools lined one side. The other side had the office door and peg-boards covered with tools. The back had stacks of pallets and boxes, opened and unopened. There wasn't anywhere visible for a cat door to fit.

"Let's look behind these shelves." Jessica got down on her designer jeaned knees and peered at the lower shelf. "Nothing here, I can see the concrete blocks. Maybe the next one." She rose to her feet in the fluid movement only someone with years of yoga could do, and moved to the next shelf.

I looked on; a bit baffled at her out-of-character actions. "Why are you doing this?"

"You need one less thing to worry about. And solving the starving cat mystery is one less."

How sweet of her to be concerned about the cat. Then it dawned on me. She believed I was in deep trouble and this was an easy way to keep my mind off things. My pleasure at being here at this sunny airfield was dimmed. And, on cue, the sun disappeared behind a cloud. The already dark hangar got even darker.

"Help me here. This is heavy." Jessica tugged at a metal tool-box.

It took the two of us and a lot of huffing and puffing to move the Snap-On tool-boxes stacked below the shelves. Our efforts revealed a piece of plywood propped up against the cinder blocks and held in place by the tool boxes. Jessica looked at her manicure, gave a shrug of regret, and pulled at the wood. It came away quite easily to reveal a large hole, at least two feet across.

"That's a really large hole. What's it for? It's too big for a pet door." She asked.

Peter's voice answered from the doorway, "It was an exhaust hole. This was a paint hangar once. Joe had it boarded up, but some animal gnawed a hole in the wood and he didn't repair it. Then Muffy arrived and took it over as his entrance."

"It was totally blocked up this time and Muffy couldn't get in. We've opened it up." I got to my feet and faced Peter.

"You shouldn't leave it like that. A skunk or even a small bear could get in." Peter came over to inspect the hole.

"I don't want Muffy out in the wet and cold. Can we make the hole smaller? Like a real cat door?" I liked Muffy and didn't want him to run away again. He and I had been friends in happier times. I must admit he'd slipped out of my mind this past year with all the mess my life was in. But now he was back I wanted him to stay. He was one of the last good connections I had with Joe and he would, hopefully, keep the mice population down.

"He's an airfield cat. He likes being outside," Peter answered.

I glowered at this unfeeling man. "No, he doesn't. He was really happy when I showed up. Did Joe drive him away?"

"I don't think so. He was hanging around a week or so ago when we had one of the Cessnas in for its annual inspection. Maria was really pissed at him. She's allergic and afraid of cats."

"I bet she made Joe board the hole up." Hearing her name made me see red…and black lingerie. "I'm going to leave it open."

"That's not a good idea. A person could fit through there." Jessica had been quiet up until now. "I think we can fashion a small opening with some wood and liquid nails."

I looked at her in amazement. "What are liquid nails?" I was less of a city girl than she, and I'd never heard of them.

"It's super strong glue. I used it to glue things on the wall in my apartment. Like the tiles from Portugal and the foundation for the window treatments. It's really good stuff."

"If it's that good, how will you get the tiles off when you move?" I asked.

"I'm not moving. That's a rent-controlled apartment."

I couldn't imagine Jessica living anywhere else but The City, but I did think she'd find a bigger, more elegant place than the cozy walk-up on the Upper West Side. "I thought you'd move to one of those new high-rises going up around Columbus Circle."

"No, I like my neighborhood. It's quiet but near enough to the action at Lincoln Center."

"Ladies, ladies. Let's get back on track. I'll fix the hole." Peter shook his head. "Boyd might have some stuff. I don't see anything here. I'll be back." He left before I could tell him that Boyd was flying.

"What's amazing about me knowing how to glue things?" Jessica dusted off her knees and inspected her manicure. She smiled with satisfaction. I assumed the coral polish was intact. "What do you want to do next? Find someone else with a motive to kill Joe or play with the cat?"

I couldn't tell if she was serious or not. I guess I'd gone a bit over-board about Muffy. Pop psychology would call it avoidance or skirting the issue. If it turned out that the airplane had been sabotaged, I was suspect *numero uno*. I glared at her. "Find Joe's killer, of course. Any thoughts of where to start?"

"None." Jessica shook her head.

I was empty of any good plans as well. I thought for a bit, then had an idea. "Dewey said something about Joe's Cessnas needing new engines. That means they were flying a lot. Engine time is counted in hours flown, not real-time. We'll go to the flight school and get the log books and leasing records for the airplanes. It'll give me an idea of the financial situation here. Let's walk, I need the exercise." I shooed Muffy out of the hangar and locked the door.

"Why'd you do that?"

"I don't want anybody in here, of course."

"I meant the shooing Muffy out bit. He can get in and out using his hole. And, it's big enough for a person to get in."

She was right. I unlocked the door and shoved the wood and toolbox against the hole. "There, no skunks or people can get in." I was annoyed at myself for not seeing the obvious. "Let's go."

High cirrus clouds now streaked the sky, I wondered if the weather was changing. I hadn't heard a forecast for ages, not since the day Joe died. How many days ago was that? Only two? So much has happened since then. For the life of me, I couldn't remember what was in store for the week ahead. Rain or shine? It didn't matter, I wasn't going flying anytime soon. I didn't have an airplane and I couldn't afford to rent one of the flight school ones, even though they belonged to Joe. No, they belong to me now. I might even end up in jail. The roar of an engine broke through my maudlin thoughts. Someone was going flying.

Jessica stopped to look. "It looks so small, like a toy."

We watched while the pilot did his run-up. The engine noise increased and the single-engine Beechcraft trembled on the edge of the runway. A shaft of sunlight winked off the spinning propeller and lit up the blue and white fuselage. Then, with a last shudder, the pilot cut back on the throttle and the airplane turned smoothly onto the runway, gathered speed, and soared into the sky halfway down the runway.

"I think I'd like to do that," Jessica said, still staring as the Beechcraft headed west and got smaller in the distance.

"I'll get Peter or Boyd to take you up." I now wished I'd spent the time to get my ticket. Two years of practicing was too much. I made a private promise that if I got rid of this cloud overhead, I'd go all out for a private pilot's license.

The joyous feeling of watching a pretty airplane take to the skies dissolved when I opened the door to the flight school. Maria was in there checking out a student. She spun around when Frank, the dispatcher said, "Hi, Mrs. Tomei. I'm so sorry about Joe. What can I do for you?"

I chickened out in the face of Maria's look of wrath. I wasn't ready for a confrontation, so I squeaked, "The ladies' room." I bolted for it, leaving Jessica to do her cool and aloof thing. Yes, I know I was a coward, but I didn't expect to see Maria there and I needed time to collect my thoughts and decide how I was going to treat her. Would it be the aggrieved and angry wife? Or the grieving widow? Or the sophisticated New Yorker and career woman who didn't care about her late husband's tawdry mistress? So many choices.

I spent more time in the bathroom than necessary and still hadn't made a decision about my reaction when I unlocked the door. It was a moot point. Maria had left. I could see her and the student outside by the airplanes. Jessica was standing with her back to the window leafing through a magazine.

I took a deep breath of relief and went to the dispatch counter. "Frank, may I get copies of the leasing records and log books for Joe's three Cessnas?"

Before he could answer, I heard the door open behind me. I tensed up, thinking Maria had come back, but it was her student. I turned back to the counter only to be interrupted by a soft *Purrup* and a furry body wound between my legs. Muffy had come in behind the student.

"Hey Muffy, you've come back." Frank leaned over the counter and looked down at the loudly purring tomcat. "Where've you been?"

Muffy meowed happily at Frank and, tail proudly erect, did another rubbing, purring circuit of my legs. Then I felt him go still and stiffen. His hackles raised and he growled. I turned to face the direction he was looking and saw Maria on the other side of the glass door that led to the apron. Our eyes locked and she opened the door. Muffy let out a loud hiss, backed up to the safety of the space between my legs and the counter kick plate.

Maria pointed to the cat and said, "Frank, I told you not to let that animal in here." She walked towards me and came to a stop way too close to me for my comfort. I took a step back and Maria closed the gap. She stabbed her finger inches away from my nose. I had a sudden urge to bite it, and it must have shown in my eyes and my open mouth, because her eyes widened and she stepped back an inch or two. Out of the corner of my eye I saw Jessica move towards us.

"Introduce us, sweetie," Jessica's cool voice rang out.

Maria didn't move. "You don't belong here. Get out." Her hiss was a very good imitation of Muffy's and he obliged by hissing back at her. "And you, shut up." She made a move to kick Muffy. But as he was still behind my legs it meant she'd kick me. I sidestepped quickly, leaving Muffy exposed. He reacted by lashing out with his claws fully extended and catching her across her scarlet pedicured big toe.

"Yeow!" I wasn't sure if the screech came from Maria or Muffy. She took another kick at him, lost her balance and stomped down on his furiously lashing tail. Now this tail had already been abused by Arnold Watson and it must still smart. Muffy took even more offense at this second assault on him, so he went into full attack mode, starting off with a yowl of range and pain. Maria jumped backward and he leaped at her khaki cargo pants and hung on for dear life.

"Get him off me. I'll kill him." Maria shook her leg

Muffy slipped off and scuttled over to hide behind Jessica. Her hand was covering her mouth, but it wasn't big enough to hide her wide grin of amusement. I guess I'd have thought the scene funny if I hadn't been part of it.

Frank, the dispatcher, wisely stayed behind the counter and kept very quiet. I noticed that the student was cowering behind the magazine rack.

Maria turned her venom on me, but wisely refrained from pointing her finger in my face this time. "You, you…Go back to New York. You don't belong here."

I shouldn't have answered her. But it was as if my mouth took over my brain. "Actually, this place belongs to me now. So yes, I do belong here."

Maria's reaction was interesting. First, she turned white, then seconds later bright red. She didn't say anything for a couple of heartbeats. Then she screamed, "You bitch. You're the one who should be dead." And lunged for my hair.

I dodged to one side and Maria followed. Jessica moved in and Muffy got down on his haunches ready to leap again. It looked like we were going to have one big cat fight. Then, out of the corner of my eye, I saw the door to the parking lot open and Demetri Balasi walk in.

"Maria, stop that." He crossed the distance between the door and Maria in two strides and pulled her off me. I was glad I'd had my hair cut short last week in defiance of Joe's preference for long, flowing locks. Maria's fingers didn't have a good hold on my two-inch-long follicles and her claws slipped off with only a small amount of pain on my end.

Balasi held tight to Maria and said, "You ladies must not fight. This is not a good time for either of you. Please make peace."

"I'm not making peace with this bitch. She comes in here saying she owns the airfield now. Well, she can't. I'll stop it." Maria struggled out of Balasi's arms and stormed out to her still-waiting student. The glass door came close to shattering from the force of her slam. I pitied that student. He was in for a bumpy ride.

Balasi looked at her retreating back, shook his head, and turned to me. "I apologize for my cousin's behavior. She is upset."

"I'm upset as well." I did not want to talk to this man. "Frank, would you get me those copies of the flight records please?"

"How far back do you want to go?"

"Since the beginning of the year. I've got to figure out…"

"Ahem…" Jessica's cough interrupted my explanation that I needed to know where the money was. "We could come back for them later, Fiona. I think we'd better get your cat out of here before he creates any more mayhem." She pointed to Muffy who was now sitting very upright and cleaning his claws. I hoped he had Maria's flesh on them, but that it didn't poison him.

For a moment I wondered why Jessica wanted us out of here. Then I looked at Balasi and realized it wasn't a good idea to let him, or anyone, know I was in financial straits.

"Mrs. Tomei. Perhaps we could discuss the business proposition I presented to you the other day. As the owner of this establishment, I'm sure you will be interested in what I have to offer." Balasi had a strange, rather formal, way of talking.

Jessica stepped forward. "Leave the proposal with us, Mr.…? What did you say your name was?"

Now I know she remembered his name, Jessica never forgot anything. She was doing her frosty lawyer thing again. She did that when she didn't like anyone, and it was obvious she didn't like Balasi.

Balasi gave her a smile. I swear I saw a gold tooth twinkle in his mouth. I wondered if he thought he could charm her. "Demetri Balasi, entrepreneur, at your service." He actually bowed. It was just a little dip from his waist, but it was still a bow.

I stifled a giggle. Many men would love to lay themselves at Jessica's feet, but bowing, was a bit much. "Yes, leave the papers with me. I'll look over them later."

"Sadly, I don't have them with me. But I could discuss it with you right now. Shall we sit down?" He pointed to the tables and chairs where the students study FAA rules and regulations, drink the flight school's disgusting coffee, and talk about flying.

Jessica took up the challenge. "Not today, Mr. Balasi. If you'd like to mail it to Fiona, she'll discuss it with her advisers."

I didn't know I had advisers, but it sounded good. Then I remembered that Bill Dewey was managing the airfield business until everything got cleared up. I was about to tell this to Balasi and send him over there when Muffy growled. What was fussing him this time? I looked out the apron door, half wondering if Maria had come back. But no. This time it was a large black Labrador. The dog had its nose pressed against the glass door. I hoped it hadn't seen Muffy since it was big enough to crash through the glass. I couldn't afford to replace that.

Muffy hissed and puffed up his fur. Poor thing, he must be getting exhausted with having to exhibit all this bravado. The dog whined and wagged its tail. Then the dog's head jerked, someone was pulling on its leash. "Oh look. It's Detective Masters. Is that his dog?" I called out to Frank who was shuffling through folders and running the copy machine.

He looked up. "Yup, that's Jackson. Detective Masters walks him every day around this time."

Balasi sucked in a breath and took a step away, putting himself out of the line of sight of the door. "Ah, look at the time. I must go. My apologies. Another appointment." he spun on his heel and abruptly left through the parking lot door opposite the apron door.

"I guess talking about his agreement with Joe wasn't that important after all," I murmured to Jessica.

"That or he doesn't like dogs or detectives," answered Jessica. "Look, the dog and Masters have walked over to the airplanes. Let's get this cat out of here before another fight starts."

I bent down and gathered the still over fluffed cat up. "Do you have those copies, Frank?"

"Yes, here they are." He held them up.

"Give them to Jessica, I'm full of cat. Thanks a million. Bye." I liked to think our exit was dignified, despite the struggling fur ball in my arms. I hoped his over-exercised claws would stay sheathed and I kept his eyes shielded from the dog. I made sure we were heading in the opposite direction of Masters and Jackson. Muffy made some strangulated meows and growls before settling down for the lift back to his food bowl.

"So, that was the other woman," Jessica said.

"Yes, that was Maria Avernus. What did you think of her?" I got no answer. I glanced over my shoulder and saw Jessica's eyes were fixed at a point over to my left shoulder. "What are you looking at?"

"Masters dog. He's acting really strangely by one of the airplanes."

"Strange, like what?" Muffy was twitching. I held him tight.

"Like a drug or arson dog does when it finds something." Jessica was now walking backward keeping an eye on the scene behind us.

"I can't look, Muffy is going to escape." I kept walking toward the hangar. "What else is happening?"

"Masters has opened the airplane door." Jessica was doing a great job of keeping up with me and walking in reverse. "Now he's looking inside without a search warrant. That takes nerve."

"Which airplane is it?"

"A little one."

"They are all little ones." I tried to look over my shoulder, but Muffy struggled again and hissed. I wanted to get him to the hangar and out of sight of the dog.

"Well, they all look the same to me. Oh, look. Peter has just shown up. He and Masters are talking." Jessica was sounding breathless.

"I can't." I knew she was in better shape than I was, and, though I was walking fast, I wasn't out of breath. They do say that walking backward is more strenuous than forward. A moment passed and then she said, "They've all gone into the flight school. Are we nearly at the hangar? I don't like this backward stuff."

"We're here. Turn around. Get the key out of my pocket."

She opened the man door and I dropped a protesting Muffy inside. He shook himself like a dog and headed over to his food bowl. I guess fighting puts an edge to one's appetite. "I'll put some more food down and then let's go. I've had enough of this place."

"What do you feel about taking all the files, ledgers, binders and Joe's computer back to the house and doing a thorough search of every scrap of paper and every file in the computer?" Jessica walked towards the office without waiting for me to agree to the idea. It was a good one, I just didn't relish the thought of trolling through Joe's life. But it had to be done, and we had nothing else to do this afternoon except rehash the accident.

"Good idea. I also want to get the laptop from Boyd."

It didn't take too long to gather everything up and pack into the car then lock up. I got into the driver's side, adjusted the mirror and seat and started up, then remembered. "Oh shit. I forgot about Peter coming back and fixing Muffy's escape hole. He's still inside and can't get out." I got out the car and Jessica followed suit.

Purrup. Muffy looked up from his food bowl. "Hey there. Just checking your secret hole." I crouched down by the shelves and saw that the tool boxes had been moved to one side. "Turn the lights on, Jessica." In the brightness of the neon lights, I could see a rough square of plywood covering most of the hole. Peter had come up with a stop-gap solution. There was a small opening, maybe just enough for Muffy in his emaciated state to squeeze through. I tentatively pulled at the plywood, and it was now attached to the cement block. I backed away from the shelf, stood up, dusted off my hands and announced, "There you go cat. You have a way in and out. Let's go. Goodbye, Muffy."

"How did Peter get in?" Jessica said as she stepped over the threshold.

"I guess he has a key. Joe trusted him. Should we ask him to come over and help look through this stuff?" I pointed to the pile on the back seat.

"No, let's look before we involve anyone else. What's going on over there?" Jessica pointed towards the flight school.

A police car partially blocked my view of the airplane, but Masters, his dog and Peter were in clear view.

"Do you want to stop and find out what's going on?" Jessica got into the driver's seat.

I thought for a second. What if it was one of Joe's Cessnas? Should I get involved? On second thoughts, no. Joe leased the airplanes to the flight school. Whatever was happening, they could handle. "No, I don't want to deal with the police today. Go the back way, to the south side to Boyd."

But Boyd wasn't back from his banner towing.

CHAPTER 10

"Ugh. This is disgusting. I can't work on this." Jessica had pulled up a chair and settled in at the little desk to do some cyber searching on Joe's computer. The bright kitchen light showed up every crumb, hairball, grease stain and anything else you could think of on the screen and keyboard. I shuddered to think what I'd touched in the dimly lit office.

"I did have some electronic cleaning things when I lived here. I'll go see if I can find them." I headed off to retrieve the box from the last place I'd put it at the back of the coat closet. A faint whiff of scent emanated from the over-stuffed closet. *Did Joe change his cologne?* It was a nice smell—fruity and fresh. Something I'd like to wear. *I must check the bathroom to see what brand it is.* I pushed the coats aside. Most were Joe's, but there were a couple of mine in there as well. One was reserved for gardening and the other a leather flight jacket. I looked good in it, but it was horribly uncomfortable, too heavy and cumbersome and I only wore it the one time when Joe gave it to me. I'd forgotten all about it. I pulled the flight jacket off the hanger to show Jessica and got another faint whiff of the scent under the stronger leather odor. I breathed into the leather jacket. This wasn't my scent, so whose was it? Breathing into leather and searching a closet are a bit like patting your head while rubbing your belly. They don't work well together and I stubbed my toe on a box in the process. I tossed the jacket onto a nearby chair for a later modeling session and checked on the box. It was too heavy to push away with my foot, so I hauled it out and dove into the back of the closet to look for the electronics cleaner. It was exactly where I'd left it. Triumphantly I backed out and came up short against the offending box. This time I looked closely at the legal document box and opened it. Manila file folders were neatly stacked inside. "Hey Jessica, look at this, Joe put a bunch of files in here." I hefted the box into the kitchen and dumped it on the counter top.

"Interesting, what are they?" Jessica grabbed the cleaner and started sanitizing the mouse, keyboard and screen.

I rifled through the tabs. "Budget, expenses and receipts. It looks mostly financial."

"You sort through those, while I dig into Joe computer files. We only scratched the surface at the hangar." She pressed the power switch. "Any idea what Joe's password might be?"

"Try *Hotshotpilot79*, or if that doesn't work, try *FlyerDude79*. Joe alternated between those two. He couldn't decide what persona he wanted to be. The 79 is his birthday."

"Bingo, he's a Flyer Dude. Okay, let's see what I've got here." Jessica bent to the screen and started scrolling.

I was torn between looking over her shoulder and delving into the files. I chose the latter. Time was running out. The weekend would be over and Jessica needed to get back to work. I knew she said she'd stay on, but it wasn't fair of me to expect that. I would get compassionate leave of a couple of days. But she'd have to use her vacation time. It was very quiet in the kitchen. The only sound was the click of the range clock as the minutes ticked by. Every now and again I'd hear the roar of an airplane skim the top of the house on final approach. The prevailing wind must have veered as they were landing from the west.

The contents of the filing box made for grim reading. The airfield was pretty much in the red with little prospect of getting out. The rental income from the flight school aircraft was negligible. And the money from hangar rents didn't cover property taxes, insurance and basic upkeep. The fuel farm brought in more money than it cost to run and that was great. But it was the only good news on the very bleak horizon. I wondered what I should do about the place. Maybe selling out was the answer. But the visual of dozens of identical houses peppering the rolling green spaces between the runway and the taxiways was abhorrent. The ultralight field would be dug up for a shopping strip. It was all too horrible to imagine. I had been happy here once. I leaned back with a deep sigh.

"What's the matter?" Jessica looked up from her work.

"The airfield is in worse shape than Bill Dewey led me to believe. I don't know what to do about it."

"First things first. We've got to figure out the mess of Joe's death."

"Is there anything in the computer?" I asked.

"I've been searching his browser history. There's not much there. Also, nothing in the files. It's all pretty clean. I've also been trying to see if there is anything online to do with the crash or Hasborough. Nothing that we haven't seen. There are some emails from people who don't know Joe is dead. Do you want me to answer any of them on your behalf?"

"Let me see if I recognize the names." I moved to look over Jessica's shoulder. "That's strange, these are all recent. There's nothing earlier than the day before he died."

"Yes, I noticed that too. I tried get his emails through the internet, but nothing. He must have downloaded them onto something," Jessica said.

"His laptop. He used that more than this."

"Didn't Boyd say he was getting a new one?"

"Yes. But where is it? It's not in this house."

"Here's an email from the computer store. The new one was due on Thursday. And, here's one from FedEx. They tried to deliver it twice. It's at their depot. Did you see a sticker on your door?"

On this information, I opened the front door. Sure enough, there was the familiar red and blue sticker. I have no idea how I missed it, but I had. I blame the oversight on all the traumatic comings and goings.

I reported this to Jessica. She had her hard thinking look on. "You know when you get a new device, most people back up the info on the old one to an external drive. Have you seen one of those around?"

I did a mental scan of all the spaces in the house and office. No little black box sprang to mind. But something niggled in the recesses of my brain. I tried to focus on it, but it slipped further and further away. I had to get the laptop.

"Maybe Boyd is back in his hangar by now." I tried his cell. No answer. Banner towing airplanes are noisy and phones can't be heard. It's also frowned upon to use cell phones when flying. So, I texted him. Who knew when he'd get it? And, what good would it do if he wasn't in the area. He could be out all day towing his banner up and down the Jersey Shore for the Indian summer beach goers. He'd have to land every few hours for fuel. But it wouldn't necessarily be at Joe's airfield.

"I need coffee. You want some?" Jessica stretched and got up to start making it.

I stacked some of the paperwork on the breakfast counter. And there it was. The catch all bowl for keys, coins and pocket contents. "The thumb drive." I squeaked in excitement and held it up.

Jessica stopped her coffee making and grabbed it from me. "Please, please let there be a port for this. She got down on her hands and knees and searched around the back of the CPU." Joe's desktop was so old it even had a floppy disc drive slot.

"Bingo. Here's one." She got up, dusted herself off and settled in to upload. "What was that password again?" I gave it to her and took up a position where I could see the screen. She scrolled down "Wait. Is that who I think it is?" I pointed to the hated name, Maria.

"Yes, it's her. Don't look. They'll upset you."

"I want to see what she wrote. Bring up all of them and what Joe answered." I pulled a stool up alongside Jessica.

"Are you sure?" Jessica looked worried.

"I'm sure. If you won't do it, I will." I was getting steamed up and hadn't even read a single one yet. Seconds later, my thermostat over-heated and I saw red. "*Studmeister*! She called him that? Yuck, that's so...." I couldn't come up with a word to describe how I felt about someone else talking about Joe's assets. He was good in bed. That's one of the reasons I stayed so long in the marriage.

"Yucky. I agree. Let's see what he calls her." Jessica seemed to have given up her concern I'd be upset. She opened up another one. "Look, *Pussywillow*. What does that mean?" She laughed.

Her laugh was contagious and despite my anger, I giggled. *Pussy-willow* was the lamest endearment I'd heard. "Does it mean her 'you know what' is pliable. Does it waft in the breeze?" I snorted.

"Don't even go there," Jessica gasped. I wasn't sure if it was laughter or disgust. "Maybe he called it that because it can search for things. You know, dowsing. Aren't willow branches used as divining rods?"

"Enough already. You're hurting me." I was bent double trying to stop the waves of laughter. I had a stitch in my side.

"Deep breaths. Be serious. We've work to do." Jessica's giggling belied her words.

"Keep looking."

We scrolled through email after email. The early ones were hot and sexy. But then Joe started slacking off on the endearments. From the tone of her replies and her pleading, you could tell Maria wasn't too happy about this. The further we read into the relationship, the happier I became. Joe was going to dump her, but she didn't know it yet. I'd been married to him long enough to read between the lines of his correspondence. He used to send me multiple emails and texts throughout the day.

"Look. This gets interesting." Jessica pointed. Maria mentioned her cousin, Demetri Balasi. He was in town, up from Florida. She wanted Joe to join them for dinner. The date on this email was two weeks ago. She said Balasi had a solution to get the airfield out of the red.

"Is there anything to say what they talked about?" I peered closer to the screen in the hope that something would materialize. "Search on Balasi's name."

"Here it is." Jessica clicked it open. "It's dated last week. Balasi wants to bring some papers over to Joe."

"So, he was right when he said Joe hadn't signed anything. Is there an attachment?" I asked.

Jessica didn't answer immediately. She continued reading, then said, "Balasi is saying that his deal is better than Hasborough's. That he will keep the place as an airfield. But if Joe sells out to developers, Watson will pave it over."

"Look for things from Watson." I was getting excited. Maybe we'd get some answers from this treasure trove of emails. I should have looked for Joe's laptop the day he died. I just didn't think about it then.

"Here they are. The first one is an inquiry about the airfield based on a recommendation by Arnold Watson's good friend, George Tomei." Jessica raised her eyebrows. "Seems your brother-in-law is interested in the airfield. I thought you said the Tomeis hated it."

"They hate what it represents. It prevented Joe from being involved in the catering and restaurant business. I'm sure they know the value of the land and they'd love to get their hands on even a small percentage of that. We're talking millions here."

The rest of the emails between Watson and Joe and George told the story of Joe refusing to consider the sale. George was pushing it. There were even some veiled threats of either George or Watson holding some tax liens on the property.

It was a lot to digest and I wished I had a printer here. I work better with things on paper. I wanted to pour over all these emails, lay them out on the dining table and think things through. I was just about to suggest that we head back to the airfield to get the printer when Jessica said, "Oh look, some from Boyd."

"Why would Boyd send Joe emails? They saw each other every day. They lunched together."

"Probably some joke. Let's look and have another laugh." She opened it.

But it wasn't a joke! I read it aloud over her shoulder. "Joe, I have a business proposition for you. I'm putting it in writing to make it formal. You need money and I need assurance that the airfield stays an airfield. I've got a lot of contracts for banner towing so I am expanding the business with more equipment. This place is the closest to getting aerial advertisements over all the major population points like along the Hudson River, New York City and the Jersey Shore. But I can't invest in more aircraft if you're selling out to developers. Let's talk about a partnership in the airfield. Boyd."

"So that's three people who are interested in getting their hands on the airfield. But that gives them all a motive to keep Joe alive, not kill him. Killing him means they have to deal with you. It doesn't make sense doctoring his fuel and killing him." Jessica rubbed her temples. "I'm getting a headache from all this."

"There's aspirin in the bathroom. Bring me two. I'm going to look in the *trash* and *sent* files." I wiggled around on the hard stool to get comfortable for a deep cyber search.

I WAS SO ENGROSSED in the story unfolding from the emails I lost track of time. I sensed Jessica going through the cardboard box beside me. She gave up and started puttering around the kitchen. It must have gotten dark outside because the next thing I noticed was the lights going on. Then the silence broke with a faint rumbling. Was it my stomach or Jessica's? I looked over to her and caught her checking me out.

"Sounds like someone is hungry," she said.

"I am. Did you find anything to eat without doing any prep work?" I couldn't remember what we'd bought the other day. I couldn't even remember how long ago we'd shopped.

"Nothing that appeals. Let's eat out." Jessica got up and stretched into full yoga sun pose, then downward dog. "Oh, that feels good. I miss the gym. I've done no exercise for days."

"Did you find out anything good in the file box?" I asked

"One thing of interest."

"What?" I wondered why she was being coy about sharing.

"I'll tell you in a moment. Did you find anything?"

"I'm getting a good picture of what is going on. He wanted to know about the flight school's use of his airplanes. He asked Maria to get him copies of the manifests."

"Aren't those what you got this morning?"

"Yes, but they don't tell me anything more than hours the flight school say each airplane has flown. I'd have to physically check out all the airplanes' Hobbs Times. That'll tell me how many hours the airplane has really flown."

Jessica looked at me and raised her eyebrows. "This is a new side of you I didn't know. You really do know a lot of stuff about airplanes. You'd be great at running the airfield."

I shrugged my shoulders, but I was secretly pleased at Jessica's praise. For want of something to say that didn't sound boastful, I said, "Joe was definitely going to dump Maria. He told her so. Then, she threatened him. You should read what she said."

"Tell me over dinner. I'm starving. Where can we eat without being eyed by all your townsfolk?"

I opted for an old-fashioned Northern Italian cuisine restaurant two towns over. It favored white damask table linen and silver bud vases. Over the course of my marriage, I'd found out that my in-laws, being from the south of Italy, cooked differently from the Italians from the north. There was some sort of culinary rivalry going on between them all and my in-laws weren't social with the northerners. I was confident that we could eat, drink, and discuss what we'd discovered without fear of it being broadcast throughout town.

CHAPTER 11

The sommelier poured our pinot grigio, then nestled it back into its silver bucket of ice. I raised my glass in a silent salute to my good friend and sleuthing partner. Jessica returned the salute, and with a mutual sigh we took our first sip. I savored the crisp tartness of this Northern Italian wine. Simultaneously we picked up our menus. It was no multi-page menu, desperately trying to cover every possible taste in cuisine, and often mixing regions with disastrous results. No, this menu was devoted to a choice of six anti-pastas, four entrées and three desserts. I anticipated each one would be lovingly and expertly cooked by the chef in the kitchen tucked discreetly away behind swinging doors.

I chose the veal loin scaloppini with porcini mushrooms. Jessica picked scossa veal parmigiana with taglierini, oil and garlic. We'd both elected to ignore our fat intake for the day yet again. To offset the rich main course, Jessica selected a healthy baby spinach salad with cranberries and almonds to start. I decided to abandon all caution and picked the baby spinach and radicchio with gorgonzola cheese. I'd noticed it being served at an adjoining table. It looked yummy. The cheese was piled so high it tumbled off the platter.

"I'll go first with my findings today." But before I could start, a hand reached over from my right side. I looked up to see our over-solicitous waiter take my napkin, and with a practiced flip and flourish, unfold it and lay it on my lap. I smiled sweetly at him. Hmmm? *Do I know you? Your face is sort of familiar.* I couldn't place it. I shrugged and continued my reporting as he glided over to Jessica and with the same panache, laid her napkin on her lap. "Joe sent Boyd an email saying he wasn't interested in a partnership because he had found a funding source. He said Boyd didn't need to worry about the airfield disappearing. He swore he'd keep it going or die in the process."

"That sounds like a premonition. What source was he talking about? Balasi's proposal?"

"I don't think so because get this...Joe sent a really stinker of an email to Maria." I couldn't hide my grin as I said this.

"Tell me, please. Share!" Jessica laughed at the pleasure in my voice

"Let's see if I can remember it word for word." I fortified myself with another sip of wine. "Here goes...*Are you crazy? That creep, your cousin Balasi is a crook. I checked up on him with some guys in Florida. He's a slime bag drug smuggler. He wants to turn my airfield into his northeast distribution point to get his poison to Newark and New York City. I don't ever want to see him on my property again. Get rid of him and stop seeing him if you want to continue on with the flight school. You'll lose your license if the feds find you mixed up with a drug ring. My guys said the feds know he's into drugs, they just can't pin anything on him, yet. The feds are going to be here. I guarantee it. I don't want to be associated with you if this is the kind of family you have.* That's the gist of it."

"Wow. Did he really write *slime bag drug smuggler?*"

"Maybe not those exact words, but that's what he meant."

"What did that last part mean about guaranteeing the feds would be there?"

"I was thinking it was what Dewey told us about getting the fed funding and having the State Troopers helicopter operation based out of here."

The ever-attentive waiter arrived with our salads and our discussion and speculation stopped for a while as we savored the fresh leaves and toppings. I offered Jessica a taste of my cheese, but she

opted to stay low-fat for this course and stuck to her dried cranberries and shaved almonds.

"Delicious." Jessica patted her mouth with her linen napkin. "I was
thinking; Joe wrote that he'd stop Maria continuing with the flight
school. Who runs it?"

"A retired airline pilot rented the building and built up the school.
But now you mention it, I heard he went south to the Virgin Islands. I
don't know who runs it now."

"Could it be Maria?"

I choked on the last bit of my radicchio. The hovering waiter came
rushing over to fill up my water glass. I managed to gasp out between
sips, "If she is, she's a goner. Peter will know. I'm calling him." But my
call went straight to voice mail. I didn't leave a message.

The waiter clearing our empty plates kept giving me sidelong
glances. He was probably worried I'd have another choking fit. I sat
quietly and tried to channel some inner peace. I didn't want to ruin
the rest of the fabulous food we'd ordered. It worked, I breathed
freely.

"Any other interesting things in the sent or delete box?" Jessica
asked.

"A few he deleted from Maria. She was apologizing for Balasi's
actions and pleading with Joe to call her. They all dated back from last
week. Apparently, she was out of town doing something. He must
have called her, because there were no answers. But there was one in
the draft folder. He might have been breaking up with her. All he
wrote was, *Maria, this isn't working.*"

The waiter again interrupted us with our entrees and a welcome
wine re-fill.

After a deep, appreciative lungful of the aroma rising from our
plates, we silently dove in. If I had been a religious person, I would
have said a prayer of thanksgiving.

"What did you find?" I managed to get out between mouthfuls of
the most succulent veal scaloppini I'd ever consumed.

Jessica swallowed her bite of veal parmigiana and took a sip of wine before answering, "Joe had a personal million-dollar life insurance policy."

This statement, delivered in Jessica's cool, clear voice made me choke on my next bite. After coughing and a mouthful of water, I managed to gasp out, "How did I miss that?"

"It was sandwiched between the property tax delinquent notices."

"Who is the beneficiary?"

"You are."

I stared at Jessica. I knew from the now flat tone of her voice that she was thinking what I was. "That's two life insurance policies that have me as the beneficiary. They give me a good motive to kill him, don't they?" My throat tightened up and my veal got tough as I masticated it around in my mouth. I couldn't swallow. I reached for my wine to ease the lump, but it was empty. Within seconds our waiter was at hand to refill our glasses. This guy was making sure we gave him a great tip.

"Yes, but you didn't have the opportunity."

"The police don't seem to believe that."

"They're just messing with you. You said Masters was a local boy and friends with the Tomeis. They're probably pressuring him to make your life miserable. Masters hasn't charged you with anything. And if he does, a good lawyer will make mincemeat out of him. He has no case."

I hoped she was right. I was feeling very vulnerable, and the television stories I watched had lots of episodes of high-handed treatment by rogue cops.

"Some dessert and coffee ladies?" The waiter's voice jerked me out of my private pity party. He'd cleared the plates and topped up our glasses with the last of the pinot grigio and I hadn't even noticed. Tempted, I looked over at Jessica and raised my eyebrows. God bless her, she answered in the way I hoped.

"I think we need something sweet. Tiramisu sounds good to me. How about you?" She asked.

It did sound good. Sugar might ease the heaviness in my chest as I contemplated explaining two life insurance policies to the police. "Yes, and espresso." The waiter glided off with our order.

"Maybe we should have ordered a sambuca as well...you know, to allay my imminent arrest fears."

"Don't be silly. Like I said, you're covered. But a sambuca sounds good." Jessica lifted her hand to signal the waiter. He came gliding back. All the waiters in this place had a familial look. They were probably related. It was a family restaurant and hiring cousins, nephews and uncles was the norm.

With the sambuca order taken care of, Jessica went on, "I'm wondering if we should show the police the emails on the thumb drive. There's a lot of stuff in there that might help with their investigation."

"You may be right. It'll point them in a direction that isn't me."

"That's what I'm thinking. We'll do it tomorrow." She leaned over the blue flame flickering on top of the sambuca and took a deep breath. "Don't you love it how the coffee bean smells when the alcohol ignites?"

I gazed at my little blue flame, fluttering like a symbol for the married part of my life. It flamed in a last gasp, sputtered and died. I squared my shoulders. *Stop it, you don't have time for melancholic thought, you've got a murder to solve.*

We sat in silence for a while, alternating between coffee, sambuca, and tiramisu. My mind drifted from one thought to another, but nothing coherent came forth.

Jessica broke the silence. "First thing tomorrow we get Joe's laptop and take it and the thumb drive to Masters. We'll show him what we found."

"I guess so."

"You don't sound convinced now."

"It's Sunday, he might not be there. And, I was thinking about two life insurance policies and how bad that makes me look. Then, what if Masters finds other stuff, things we haven't found. The police can do this deep computer forensic stuff."

"You've been watching too much *Castle* and other cop shows on television. Don't worry, you'll be alright. We'll sleep on it and decide in the morning. If he's not there, we'll still get brownie points for being helpful."

"We should go. We're the last ones here." I looked around the dining room and signaled our hovering waiter.

"I can't believe we're closing the place. How late is it?"

"Not late, but they roll the sidewalks up early in this part of New Jersey." I left a good tip; the waiter had been very attentive.

"Who's that?" I stopped the car outside the neighbor's house and pointed to the dark figure standing in the shadows by the front door of my house.

"Do muggers ply their trade in this town?" Jessica, the quintessential city woman, sees a mugger in every shadow.

"He's not standing behind a bush or anything like that. I doubt it's a mugger." I eased the car forward and turned sharply into the driveway, switching on my high beams at the same time. The shadow became Peter Ward.

"I've been trying to reach you all evening. Don't you answer your phone?" He said as soon as we slammed the car doors shut.

"Well neither do you," I retorted, pulling my phone out of my purse. "Oops mine is in silent mode."

Peter shook his head and though it was too dark to see, I bet he rolled his eyes. "Masters' dog sniffed some drugs in Joe's rental airplane. He got upset when he found you had taken the leasing records. He wants to see them. He's been trying to reach you."

"We only took a copy. The originals are still in the flight school," Jessica said.

"No they're not. Are you sure you didn't pick up both by mistake?" Peter retorted.

"I am sure. I don't like your tone, Peter. Why are you acting as Masters' errand boy?" The words went straight from my brain to my mouth. As soon as I heard them, I knew it was a mistake. I couldn't see the expression on Peter's face, but the stiffening of his shoulders told me I was being rude. It was the pinot grigio and Sambuca talking. I liked Peter, but I was getting tired of being hounded. I remembered the expression on his face when he confronted me with the plastic baggies he and the police found in my car. It wasn't a look like, *Fiona, I know these aren't yours.* It was a look like, *I can't believe you had these in your car.* But I didn't need to make more enemies in town, so I bit my tongue and said, "I'm sorry. They're inside. Come in, you can see for yourself we only took copies." I unlocked the door and turned on the lights. Peter followed us in without saying a word.

The bright overhead light highlighted the work we'd been doing all afternoon.

"What have you two been up to?" Peter eyed the pile of files and computer on the counter and moved towards them.

"Just checking on things," Jessica spoke up and eased in to stand between the counter and Peter, effectively blocking his way. It was obvious from the look on his face that he understood her move.

To alleviate the building tension, I grabbed the leasing records and flipped some pages. "Which airplane was it?" I could never remember Joe's tail numbers.

"The Cessna 172. Foxtrot Unicorn." Peter gave the airplane's tail number. "Let me look." He looked over my shoulder. "Hold it closer to the light, I can't see."

I laughed. "You're getting old, Peter, you need glasses." This time I could see his frown, along with the same stiffening of shoulders.

"No, my arms are just getting shorter." He retorted. "Hold it still. No. give it to me." He took the papers from me and ran his fingers down the columns. "Balasi rented it a few times. Maria was pilot in command. She must be giving him flying lessons."

"I thought you said he owned an aircraft business in Florida. Isn't he a pilot?" I asked.

"I guess not. Not all owners can fly."

"You're on this too, Peter." Jessica pointed to his name on the sheet.

"Yeah. But I don't smuggle drugs." He still looked annoyed. Jessica and I weren't making any friends here tonight. "It's late. I'll drop it off at Masters' first thing in the morning." He shuffled the papers into the folder.

"No need Peter. Jessica and I can take it. We're going to see him anyhow." I slapped my hand onto the file and got a good grip and scooped it away.

Peter glowered at my move. "What about? I thought you'd had enough of him."

"Oh, just some stuff we found here." Jessica gestured towards the countertop.

"What stuff?"

"As you said, it's late. I'm tired and I'm sure Jessica is too. Goodnight, Peter."

"Yes, goodnight, Peter." Jessica did one of her socialite moves of opening her arms wide to usher him towards the door. It worked.

He involuntarily took a step backward and started to turn. Then he stopped and looked from Jessica to me. His eyes narrowed. I could see indecision in his eyes. I wondered what was going through his mind. Then he shrugged and waved his hand in a silent goodbye and went through the door.

"Why were we being nasty to Peter?" I asked when I heard his car start up.

"I'm not sure. But I'm at the stage when I'm not trusting anyone. He's one of the people who leased Joe's airplane. What do you know about him?"

"Just that he's an old friend of Joe's and a retired cop."

"He's friends with Masters as well, isn't he? I'm not even sure going to Masters is such a good idea after all."

"You might be right. But I need sleep. Can this wait until the morning?" I yawned.

"Yes. My brain is sluggish after all that food. Goodnight."

I made sure that all the windows, and back and front doors were securely locked. I reinforced my decision to get the locksmith by scribbling a note and sticking it on the fridge. In a surge of energy and effort to cross one more thing off my 'to-do' list, I hauled the box filled with old papers to the front door for Monday recycle pickup. "A reminder to get it curbside tomorrow night," I announced to the empty room. Jessica had wisely got into the bathroom first. With one last look around I turned off the lights.

SOMETHING WOKE ME. I shot upright in bed. My sleep had been so deep, I was disorientated. For a moment, I couldn't figure out where I was or why I was in this, sort of familiar, place. I wasn't in my small bed in my tiny room in Manhattan. The darkness here was too dense. In New York, the streetlights shone in no matter how much I tried to black them out. Here a velvety blackness enveloped me. The next noise brought me fully awake and aware of my surroundings. I could see a glimmer of light flickering beyond my bedroom door. I eased myself quietly out of bed, then I realized I didn't have a robe. The idea of confronting an intruder clad only in Joe's old T-shirt and underpants wasn't appealing. But waiting in bed for whoever was lurking around out there to come in and find me was even less appealing. T-shirt and underpants would have to suffice. I crept to the door and hallway and held my breath in the hope of hearing another sound coming from an identifiable direction. I heard nothing. It was as if the whole house waited on bated breath. Then I felt a presence near me and heard breathing. I sucked in a breath, *OMG, it was standing right by me. Where is the light switch?* I ran my hand along the wall praying I'd feel it. It crossed my mind that I was an idiot to be out here without a weapon, but it was too late to do anything about it now, and anyhow, I didn't own a weapon. My hand felt the switch. I took in another deep, silent breath and braced myself for whatever it was I'd confront in the light. *Ready, breathe.* A hand touched my hand. I shrieked and flipped on the switch at the same time.

"Jessica?"

"Fiona?"

Nose to nose, we eyed each other for a nano-second. Before I could gain control of my breathing and pounding heart, a loud clatter from the living room jerked both our heads around. We moved as one towards the noise. This time I found the living room switch on my first try and flooded the place with light. The front door was swinging widely on its hinges.

Side by side, standing in the doorway between the bedroom hall and the living room. we swung our heads to and fro in unison scanning the room.

"I don't see anyone," I whispered.

"Be careful. They could be in hiding."

Holding hands, we crept towards the door.

"Why are we creeping?" Jessica asked.

"Why are we holding hands?"

"Why are you whispering?"

We kept on creeping and holding hands until we'd searched the whole house. This didn't take long. If the front door hadn't been swinging in the breeze, and the fact that Jessica also heard the noise, I would have wondered if I'd dreamt the whole thing. I let go of Jessica's hand and straightened up from my semi-crouch, creeping posture. "What happened?"

"Look. Whoever it was fell over the recyclables." Jessica pointed to the overturned cardboard box.

"That's what must have woken me."

"Me too. Did they take anything?"

I looked around. It all seemed just as we'd left it, except for the open door. The breakfast counter dividing the living space from the kitchen was still cluttered with Joe's filing box and loose papers. The cushions on the couch were in the same disarray, propped up for comfortable television viewing. My purse was on the coffee table and Jessica's was by the computer on the desk in the far corner. My eyes scanned the room over and over. There was something different, but I couldn't put my finger on it. A cold draft reminded me that the front door was still open. I poked my head out to check the front porch. The halo from the street light didn't reveal much. There weren't any cars parked on the street and I couldn't see anyone lurking around.

There was no way I was going to venture further out to check. The crisp night air held the remnants of a vaguely familiar scent. I closed and relocked the front door. I sniffed the air in the house, again taking in the scent. My sleep fogged brain seemed to feel it was important to identify the source. But memory failed me.

"Why are you sniffing around like a bloodhound?"

"It's this smell, I know it."

Jessica took a sniff and shook her head. "I can't place it." This was noteworthy as Jessica Feinstein was famous for being able to name a perfume with just one sniff. "It has some fruit undertones. Maybe it comes from a tree outside."

"It's the wrong time of year for fruit trees. You're such a city girl."

"Are you sure you locked it last night? You'd had a bit to drink." Was this Jessica being snarky over my comments about being a city girl?

"I locked it." My words came out sharper than I wanted. I couldn't afford to fight with my only ally. I hoped she realized it was fear and lack of sleep talking. I wondered what to do next. I checked the frame. The door hadn't been forced. It had been opened with a key.

"Come with me. I'm going to check all the windows." Hand in hand again, we checked everything.

"We should call the police." I said without much conviction. The thought of facing Masters was very off-putting.

"Yes, we should. But do we want them here asking questions at this time of night?" Jessica seemed even less inclined than I.

"What time is it?"

"Four in the morning. I need coffee if we're dealing with the police. And I have to get dressed."

"That decides it. No police. I'll make some hot chocolate and we'll deal with the authorities in the morning."

"Good plan." Jessica filled the kettle.

"First thing in the morning I get the locksmith. Too many people have keys to Joe's places." I pulled mugs and chocolate mix out of the cabinet.

"It's Sunday. A locksmith will be expensive."

"I don't care. I'll pay the emergency price. I'm also changing the airfield locks. I've had enough of people sneaking up on me. I can afford it. Remember, I'm a prospective millionaire now." My little laugh sounded fake and hollow even to me. Heaven knows what Jessica thought. I looked at Jessica trying to gauge her reaction.

"Don't count your chickens." She gave me a wink and a small smile.

I was back to feeling hounded. Glumly I sipped at my hot chocolate. My usual 'go to' comfort food didn't help one bit.

CHAPTER 12

tried to sleep for the few remaining hours of the night, but it was no good. My mind raced like a hamster on a wheel. About seven o'clock I heard noises. *Not again. Hasn't the idiot done enough?* I fought my legs free of the tangle of sheets and prepared for battle. Then I heard the soft clink of china and cutlery. This, reinforced by the smell of brewing coffee, told me the noises were friendly. They were. Jessica, bless her, was making breakfast. And, even though we'd had hot chocolate only a few hours ago, I was hungry. My stomach must have stretched out with all the food I'd been eating these past days. You'd think a new widow and murder suspect would lose her appetite. But not me, I was in danger of gaining weight over all this.

I showered and dressed, and in the process realized that I had to buy some essential clothing. Yet another thing to add to my mental to-do list. Maybe writing things down would help me to remember them all. I did remember the locksmith. After last night, there was no way I was going to forget that chore.

"Good morning."

"Good morning to you. Coffee smells good. Ooh, you made pancakes."

"After the night we had, I think we deserve something good.

Yoghurt didn't appeal to me this morning." Jessica was, as always, impeccably turned out in a very chic looking khaki chinos and white T-shirt ensemble. More suited to a day in The Hamptons than small-town New Jersey. My limited wardrobe of jeans and Joe's old shirts looked scruffy in comparison. I grabbed the note from the fridge and wrote under *locksmith, buy clothes.*

"What are you writing?"

"My to-do list. So far, I've got locksmith and clothes shopping. What else?"

"Police."

"Yeah, I know. But do we want to report the break in? The thought of Masters poking around here annoys me."

"We promised Peter we'd take in the leasing reports this morning."

"Oh darn. I'd forgotten about those. I tell you; my brain is like a sieve. It can't hold onto anything. It is in overload mode." I added *leasing reports* and *police* to the list. "And, I didn't ask Peter who runs the flight school now."

"Don't forget all the emails on Joe's laptop," Jessica said.

I wrote that down. "I guess we'd also better mention the break-in." I stared at my pancakes and forked them around the plate. My appetite had deserted me. It looked like my day was going to be spent at the police station. Not a happy thought. I said as much to Jessica.

"Locksmith is the first on the list. Put the call in. I'll clear up here." She gathered up the plates. I noticed she hadn't finished her pancakes either.

The locksmith returned my emergency message immediately. I guess my words, "I've had a break in." did the trick. He said he'd be right over. And, sure enough, fifteen minutes later the doorbell rang. His first words were a big 'thank you' for an excuse to get away from a houseful of out-of-town in-laws.

I felt much better about taking up his Sunday with my fears of more intrusions. I pushed away the thought that we were tampering with the evidence and that Masters would tear strips off me for doing it. But I did ask the locksmith if he thought anyone had picked the lock. He assured me nobody had broken in. He said the only way into the house had been by someone with their own set of keys. This confirmation of my fears that there were multiple sets of keys to my home and hangar made me feel very vulnerable.

Locks changed on all doors and garage and a courtesy check on the security latches on the windows made me feel better. Then, just as we were all about to leave for the airfield to change those locks, the locksmith got an emergency call from someone shut out of their house. He promised to meet us at the airfield in an hour. I told him his in-laws were not going to be happy about this. He laughed and assured me that it was enough that he was happy and he'd be on his best behavior when he got home.

"I can't imagine a Manhattan locksmith acting like that," Jessica observed.

"Small-town is different from city. I kind of miss it sometimes. But other times, people can get too much into your business. I can't make up my mind which I like best."

"So, what now? Masters and the flight logs?" Jessica asked.

"Let's go shopping. Masters is probably doing some church or Sunday morning family thing and won't be at the station. He can wait until later. I need underwear, shirts and slacks. *Target* and *Walmart* might be open by now." I grabbed my purse, keys and phone and headed to the car.

"Come on, it won't kill you to go through the doors of a *Walmart*." I tossed over my shoulder at Jessica's nose wrinkle of distaste at the thought of clothes shopping at Wally's World.

"It might. For my sake, try *Target* first. It's a tad more upscale." Jessica smiled and winked.

I laughed. It's wonderful what accomplishing even half a chore and the prospect of a shopping spree with a good friend and consummate shopper can do to lift a person's mood.

We were first through the doors when *Target* opened. I threw some underpants into my cart and turned to get Jessica's verdict on a multi-hued green and blue over-blouse. But she'd disappeared. A quick look through the carousels of tops, revealed her searching the racks of work-out clothes.

"There are some terrific bargains here," She said, struggling to hold up an armful of leggings, tank-tops, sports bras and tees. "Don't tell anyone at the gym that I bought them at *Target*."

I shook my head in amazement. The stigma of shopping in a big box store couldn't beat a bargain on clothes. Jessica was a happy camper now. "Come and help me get the rest of my things, and then we're done." I laughed.

We spent a happy half hour picking out my new wardrobe and headed to the checkout. So far, the morning had gone well. Next stop airfield. Now there were two things off my 'to-do' list.

THE HANGAR MAN door was swinging gently in the breeze. "Damn, I know I locked it. I remember double-checking." I stopped the car and hopped out. Jessica followed. We cautiously, and I hope quietly, eased up to the door. I popped my head through the small opening and tried to make out the shapes in the dark empty space. I could feel Jessica breathing down my neck.

"Be careful." Her whispered and unnecessary comment didn't help. After last night, I was going to be very, very careful. "Can you see anything?"

Purrup. The soft, furry body of Muffy bumped against the back of my legs. I jumped, caught my foot on the threshold, and tumbled into the hangar.

"Are you alright? Jessica peeked around the door jamb.

"Damn you cat. You scared me." Muffy's nose was pressed against mine. "I'll probably get a bruise, but other than that, I'm good."

"Look, the office door is open." Jessica pointed over my shoulder.

I peered into the gloom. Her eyes must be sharper than mine. Then, as my eyes got accustomed to the dimness, I made out the open door. I knew I'd locked that one as well.

"Where's the light switch?" Jessica had now stepped over the threshold and was standing beside me.

"Over there, on the side wall." I pointed in the opposite direction of the office. Whoever had designed this hangar didn't have the common sense to put the light switch in a convenient position. Jessica moved carefully along the big metal doors towards the switch. Click, suddenly the hangar was flooded with cold, blue fluorescent light. I sprinted across the concrete floor. In hindsight, I know I should have been concerned that the intruder was still inside the office waiting to pounce on us. But I was too angry to worry about that. I was tired of feeling violated. I lucked out. There wasn't anyone lurking in the shadows. There was a faint, and familiar scent lingering in the office. All the drawers and the steel cabinet doors were open and the few things on the desk were not where I'd left them.

"This time, we've got to tell the police." Jessica put her arm around my shoulders. "This is not a coincidence. Two of Joe's places being broken into during the same night."

"I will. But first, I want the locks changed. I'm not leaving this place unattended."

We checked around. It was difficult to see if anything was missing. I thought the maintenance binders were still in the same position on the shelves as when we'd left. I hadn't paid much attention to them or to the customer files. They too were still in alphabetic order and full of papers. But again, I hadn't looked, so didn't know if they'd been tampered with. The business files were at the house, along with the desktop computer. I wished I'd brought them with us. I could protect whatever was in them if I didn't let them out of my sight. But, in the rush to get to the store before the locksmith made it to the airfield, I'd left them behind.

"What are they looking for?" I sank into Joe's chair and put my head in my hands.

"The computer or laptop. There's something in there that we haven't seen, and it's important to them. Someone was in here right after Joe's crash and took the contents of the real estate file. I guess they realized there might be more stuff on the computer. Maybe they didn't know where the laptop was," Jessica answered.

"Joe usually took it with him everywhere, even flying."

"This time though, he left it at Boyd's place."

"I'm calling him now."

Boyd answered on the first ring. I was a little surprised, as I thought he might be doing another banner towing trip. Then I found out why he was still on the ground. His hangar had been broken into and the only things missing were his and Joe's laptops. Boyd was more than annoyed and said the police were on their way. I mentioned I'd also had a break-in.

"Well so much for avoiding the police this morning," Jessica said after I relayed this information to her. "The key to all of this is the laptop. We didn't finish checking everything. There must be something really big and incriminating in there."

The loud clamor of my phone interrupted us.

"Fiona, where are you? Why aren't you here at the police station?" It was Peter and he sounded annoyed.

"I had something important to take care of." Two can play the sounding annoyed game.

"Like what? Those leasing records are important. Masters is bringing Balasi in for questioning about the drugs in the airplane and he needs them."

I raised my eyebrows at Jessica who was leaning in to listen to both sides of the conversation. Had she brought the leasing agreements with her? I know I hadn't. She shrugged her shoulders in what I took for a 'no.' I mouthed, 'what shall I tell him?' All I got was another shrug.

"Hello. Are you still there Fiona?" I guess Peter was worried about the long silence. "Where are you anyhow?"

"Why are you two still here?" The deep, guttural voice from the door made me jump a mile and I dropped my phone. It surprised Jessica too, as she jerked her head around so fast her hair flipped me in the face. George Tomei glowered at us from the office door.

"Hello, George. How nice to see you." I hoped he sensed the sarcasm, but I doubted it would penetrate his dense skull.

"Fiona, Fiona. Where are you?" Peter's voice shouted from the phone.

"At the airfield, Peter. The police are coming out here. Got to go. I'll see you later." I hung up on him. I could only deal with one demanding male at a time.

"Why shouldn't we be here?" Jessica's voice was saccharine.

"This is a Tomei business. Not yours." George jabbed his finger in her direction.

I could feel my blood pressure rising. How dare this toad be rude to my friend? "I'm a Tomei, George. And this is my business now. What are you doing here?"

His eyes widened at the question. George didn't often have people talk back at him. He had no reason to be at the airfield. He'd often told Joe it was a waste of time and money.

"I saw the hangar door open. Maybe someone was making trouble in here," he muttered.

"Someone did break in here last night. Was that you, George?" I couldn't quite believe Jessica asked him this. She was probably angry at having a finger pointed at her. Even so, George was intimidating and I avoided confrontation most of the time I was around him.

"Why would I break in here?"

"Maybe something to do with Hasborough?" Jessica said.

"What the hell?" George again looked startled and took a step backward. "How do you know about that?"

"We saw the files and met Arnold Watson," I noted with satisfaction how uncomfortable George seemed.

"So what?" He sputtered. "That's a legitimate deal. It'll make a lot of money."

"Joe didn't want to do it," I said.

"That doesn't matter now. It's going to happen."

"Not if I can help it." I struggled to keep my voice steady, though I was losing my cool.

"How are you going to stop it?" He sneered.

"It's my airfield now. I can do what I want." I had a strong urge to stamp my foot but refrained. That would have been too childish and I didn't want to cede ground to George. This argument was sliding into kindergarten playground territory.

"Who says it's your airfield?"

"Joe's last will and testament says it."

"When did you see that?"

I took a step back at the murderous look in George's eyes when he said this. I was glad the desk stood between us. Jessica also took a step back. This man was dangerous.

"Hey, Fiona. You okay? Peter told me you had a visitor." I was never so glad to see Chuck Boyd standing in the doorway.

George spun around. "You...you get out of here." He actually hissed and pointed his finger at Boyd. I didn't think grown men did things like this.

"Hey, what the hell is the matter with you? Look, I'm sorry for you losing your brother. But he was my best friend. No need to act that way."

"You think that because you were Joe's friend, he'd go into partnership with you. Well, he wasn't going to do that. He couldn't." Spittle was forming in the corners of George's mouth.

"What do you mean 'couldn't'? Anyhow Joe's dead. I'll deal with the new owner."

"I got the tax liens on this place. I'm the new owner." George hissed again.

"Excuse me. You forget. Fiona inherits it all." Jessica spoke up from the corner of the now over-crowded office. "You owning the tax liens means nothing. She can pay them off."

"We'll see about that. She's got no money." George took the two steps to the door, making Boyd step smartly out of his way. With one hand on the doorjamb, he turned and glared at me. "People are saying the crash wasn't an accident. They say the airplane was sabotaged."

My heart sank. Someone was spreading the word around town about the water in the tank. "Who told you this?"

"My sources. This is my town. You're a stranger here. There's talk you killed my brother." George had let go of the doorjamb and had made a move back into the office. The look on his face scared me.

"I wasn't here when Joe took off." The marriage counselor would be my alibi.

"I heard you were here early on. You want this place for yourself. You'd have nothing with a divorce."

"You're crazy, demented. You hated Joe and this airfield." The incendiary words flew out of my mouth and hung in the stale office air. I wished I could retract them. George looked ready to explode.

"Crazy? You're calling me crazy?" He took a step towards me.

I took an involuntary step backward even though there was a desk between him and me. Then, all hell broke loose.

"Yeow" I felt something soft under my heel. It was Muffy's poor tail again.

"Muffy, poor baby. I'm sorry." I stooped and gathered the irate feline into my arms. He hissed and spat and leaped out of my arms, bounced on the desk, and ran straight for George, who promptly jumped to the side and cannoned into Boyd.

"Hey, watch out, man." Boyd was backed up against the wall.

"Get out of my way," George yelled.

"You're the one who's moving." Boyd pushed George away.

"Don't touch me. She hired you to kill my brother." George spun around and elbowed Boyd in the gut, then pointed his finger at me.

"You're crazy." Oops. I used that word again and from the look on George's face, he heard it.

"You're not getting this airfield. And you're going to fry for Joe's death." The fat finger jabbed in my direction again. "Don't show up at the funeral. My mother doesn't want you there." Then he abruptly turned and left.

"Dear god, that man is demented," Jessica said into the silence.

"He is that. If he's spreading rumors that I sabotaged Joe's airplane, I'll kill him." Boyd was red with indignation. "I'm going to O'Brady's to check out what people are saying."

"Isn't it a little early to start drinking?" Jessica asked.

"I'm flying this afternoon." Boyd glowered at her.

"So?" Jessica looked puzzled.

"What Boyd means is that he won't drink alcohol until after he stops flying for the day. The rule is *eight hours from bottle to throttle.* A pilot will lose his license if he takes a drink and flies. O'Brady's does a good business in coffee for the flyboys." I looked at Boyd while I was explaining the nuances of the world of aviation to Jessica. I suppressed a giggle at his unmanly eye-rolling. He caught me looking, shrugged in obvious exasperation, and left the office.

I stared at his retreating back and wondered a bit about his churlishness. Was he really worried George would ruin his reputation? Chuck Boyd was a good friend of Joe's, and I'm sure everyone in town knew this. Why would he be afraid of what people said behind his back?

"Boyd, what did the police say about your break-in?" I called after him.

"They're still there. I've got to get back to them." He said over his shoulder as he stepped over the threshold. The sound of the door closing behind him echoed across the cavernous space.

"Is there any credence to what George said? Could Boyd have doctored Joe's fuel? Not on your orders, of course. But, on his own. He did want part of the airfield. Maybe he knew that you were a softer touch than Joe and he could sweet talk you into a partnership with Joe out the way."

"No, I don't believe that for a moment. Chuck Boyd is the sweetest, gentlest person I know. He'd never harm anyone."

"Calm down. I didn't mean to upset you. I'm just trying to look at things from all angles." Jessica reached over and touched my arm.

"I'm sorry. I didn't mean to snap. This whole business is getting to me. Where is that locksmith? I'm sick of being cooped up here waiting." I dumped some cat food into Muffy's dish as a peace offering. "And, I need to pee."

"Me too. Can we safely leave the hangar for a few minutes?" Jessica stood up.

"I guess so. There's nothing left here to take now. Whoever was here had all night to find what they were looking for. Let's get out of here before the police come over. I'll leave a note for the locksmith that we are at the flight school and will be back in five or ten minutes. We'll take the car since it'll save time."

CHAPTER 13

I didn't know the young dispatcher manning the flight school information desk. He didn't look up when we slipped in to use the ladies' room. I guess he was used to pilots coming in off the flight line, usually desperate to use the facilities after a five-hour, bathroom-less, journey.

Nature's call over, I approached the desk to introduce myself. I might as well get my name out there as I was now, supposedly, the new owner of the airfield.

"Hi there, I don't think we've met. I'm Mrs. Fiona Tomei." I'm not sure why I used the honorific. Maybe I was establishing ownership.

The dispatcher's head jerked up and his eyebrows disappeared into his over-long brown hair. "Mrs. Tomei?" His voice boomed around the room. "You're Joe's wife?"

"Yes, is that surprising?"

"No. Yes. I'm sorry," He stood up and his eyes did a one-eighty around the flight school then homed in on me. "Ma'am. Please, I'm sorry."

I wondered if he was going to keep on saying he was sorry. For what, I didn't know. He looked like a kid caught with his hand in the cookie jar. I had to put him at ease, but I didn't quite know what was wrong or what to say.

"Ma'am, please accept my condolences on your loss." He extended his hand to me, even though his eyes were still darting around the room. I had a feeling he was looking for someone, and he was afraid of this person.

"Thank you. However, don't call me Ma'am. If we're going to be working together…"

"Working together?" His voice went up a couple of octaves. Was it surprise or was he so young his voice hadn't changed? He must be still in his teens. He still had some acne and his attempt at a soul patch was only a dream of a beard to come.

Jessica took pity on him and stepped forward. "Hi, my name is Jessica. What's yours?"

He dragged his eyes away from my face and gaped at Jessica. By the visible squaring of his shoulders, I surmised he wasn't too young to be wowed by her beauty. Sometimes I wished I could get that kind of reaction from the male species.

"Jimmy. My name is Jimmy."

"Pleased to meet you, Jimmy. Now tell me, why are you acting so surprised by Fiona's presence?"

"It's just that…" Jimmy took a deep breath and went into silent mode.

"What?" Jessica prompted him. His mouth opened and shut like a landed fish.

Poor Jimmy focused again on me and found his voice, "I didn't expect to ever really meet you, even though we have sort of met. Three days ago, the morning of the accident."

The memory of that day flooded back. Was it only three days? "Oh, you were at the crash scene."

Jimmy looked very uncomfortable. His eyes were doing their search of the room again. But this time they came to a halt at something behind Jessica and me and opened wide. I turned in time to see a flash of long dark hair disappear from the glass door. Next moment I saw the school's golf cart move away at what could possibly be top speed for the antiquated and battered vehicle.

Jessica moved to the window. "Wow, she's pulling a donut in a buggy. Oooh, she nearly tipped over."

I moved to stand beside her just in time to see the golf cart disappear behind the hangars. I turned back to Jimmy, who was looking decidedly uncomfortable.

"Who was that, Jimmy?"

"I dunno."

From the deer in-the-headlights look in his eyes, I wasn't convinced he didn't know. But I let this go for the moment. I was more interested in why Jimmy was surprised at my presence. "So, you were telling me how we met."

At this the poor kid looked even more wretched, but he answered, "On the phone. You called to schedule a lesson with Peter."

"Oh, so it was you I talked to. But that still doesn't explain your surprise at seeing me." I felt like I was doing a Spanish Inquisition on the poor guy. But his whole attitude had made me curious. Then I had a flash of inspiration. "Was Joe here when I called?"

"Not then." He shifted uncomfortably.

"But later?" Jessica prompted.

"Yes. He came in as I was calling Peter to tell him about the lesson." Jimmy's Adam's apple bobbed up and down.

I felt sorry for him but still didn't get why he was so nervous. "What was Joe's reaction to me wanting to fly his Super Cub?"

"He…he was okay with it." He paused and took a deep breath, "But, Maria wasn't."

I willed myself to not let my reaction show at this pronouncement. I could feel the hair at my nape rise at the thought of Joe and Maria discussing me. I breathed deeply and focused on the kid. It wasn't Jimmy's problem and if I wanted information from him, I'd have to stay calm.

"What did she say or do?" Jessica got the questions out before I did and gave me time to cool down.

Jimmy's eyes darted from side to side, managing to avoid looking at either of us.

"Was Maria unhappy about Fiona flying Joe's airplane?" Jessica prompted him.

He nodded his head.

I leaned over the glass counter filled with aeronautical charts, headsets, flight calculators, and log books. Jimmy took a step back. I wondered what he thought I was going to do to him. I did have an urge to throttle the answer out of him. "What did Maria do?"

Jimmy gulped. "She threw a fit." He heaved a big sigh, sat down in his chair, and looked up at us. Poor kid, I was sorry for him. He had three women on his ass. Two right here in the room, and the other here by inference.

"Go on," I said. "What happened?"

"Are you really going to be the new owner of the airfield?" You could see Jimmy weighing the options in his mind. Be nice to the new owner or be nice to the remnants of the old regime? The choice made, he started talking fast. "Maria accused Joe of being unfaithful to her. She said he'd promised to marry her. She said you had no rights to the Super Cub. She called him a wimp and that he was going back on their plan to make changes at the airfield. Joe got mad back at her and said he was still married. That's all."

"What do you mean, that's all?" Jessica's reaction matched mine. We wanted more.

"They took the argument outside. I couldn't hear anything. But their arms were waving around and Joe stormed off towards his hangar. A short time later he pulled the Super Cub around to the front with the tug."

I would have given anything to have been a fly on the wall during that argument. "What did Maria do?"

"She came back inside. She was still yelling things like..." He looked at me, took a deep breath, and went on, "I'll get that bitch. I'm Joe's fiancée. The airfield's mine. I'll show her. Then she left." Jimmy sat back in his chair and tugged at his soul patch. He looked relieved to have gotten it all out. "Please don't say anything to Maria. She'll kill me."

Jessica and I stared at him. *That was some outburst. But what did it explain?* "Thanks for telling me. Don't worry about Maria. I'll see she doesn't mess with you."

Jessica nudged me. "We should go back to the hangar. The locksmith might be there."

"We'd have seen him drive by. But you're right. See you, Jimmy." I waved cheerily at the kid. He looked shell-shocked. *I'll keep him on. I think I won his loyalty. And Jessica had definitely won his heart.* He waved rather feebly back at us. I got the impression he was relieved to see us leave.

The man door banged back and forth in the wind. The block of wood I'd used to prop it shut lay on the ground. There was no way of telling if it had fallen from natural forces, or if someone had kicked it away. The note for the locksmith wasn't there either. We peered cautiously through the opening before venturing into the cavernous interior.

Purrup. Muffy hopped over the threshold behind us and went over to his food bowl. He shot me a glowering look when he saw it was still empty.

"Later cat. You've already had one meal this morning. You'll bankrupt me at the rate you want to eat. Stop pushing it. Moving it around won't magically fill it up."

I followed Jessica to the office leaving Muffy sniffing around the floor in the hopes he'd find a stray morsel. I noticed that Jessica eased the office door open and peeked inside before entering. I guess she was feeling as cautious as I was about intruders. With this thought, I moved quickly across the hangar floor only to be brought to a halt by a loud snarl and hiss from Muffy. I turned to see he'd doubled in size; his tail was straight up in the hair and puffed out for maximum scare-value. His eyes had narrowed into slits and were fixated on the man door. He gave out another hiss for good measure.

"What's the matter? I told you, no more food. Stop trying to scare me."

Then I heard a car door slam. "Silly, it's only the locksmith." I walked back to the man door ignoring my over-fluffed and still hissing cat.

The first thing to greet me was a large hound. *Oh no. Not Masters already. I guess the police have heard about my break-in from Boyd.*

"Jessica, we have company." I wasn't going to face the detective alone. I wanted my friend's man-destroying looks to diffuse the tension. However, it wasn't Masters who held the other end of the leash. "What are you doing with the dog, Peter?"

"Masters is over at Boyd's hangar checking out that break-in. But he also wants the flight school log. The dog was getting restless so I volunteered to exercise it and get them. And I was kind of worried that George was still here bugging you. So here I am getting brownie points all around." Peter smiled triumphantly while the dog panted at his side.

Muffy must have decided that the dog was a mortal threat to his existence. So, instead of being quiet and slinking away, he let out a yowl and bolted to his escape hole. Masters' dog gave a delighted bark and lunged forward, pulling the leash from Peter's hand. With another bark, it leapt over the threshold in hot pursuit. Muffy scrabbled and clawed his way through the shelves to his hole. But he was out of luck. Peter had underestimated Muffy's size and he couldn't squeeze through the gap. He growled in frustration when he saw the boards blocking his escape. He leapt onto the next shelf up and turned to face his enemy. Every hair on his body stood out at right angles. He was a huge orange fur-ball.

"Stop the dog, Peter." I ran towards the cat, hoping to get between the hound and the now spitting, bristling and snarling feline.

Peter lunged for the dog, but it was too quick for him. It put its front paws on the second shelf and woofed in joy. Muffy was only inches away from the big yellow teeth. He couldn't go up one more shelf as his path or trajectory was blocked. So, he took the only escape route available to him. Unfortunately, this involved using my body as a trampoline. He gathered himself up for the leap, launched into the air, hit my chest with a breath-destroying thud and clawed his way up onto my shoulder. There he wound himself around my neck and hissed at the dog and the world.

My immediate fear was that the dog would follow Muffy up my body. But strangely, it turned away from me and started sniffing the shelves in front of the soon-to-be cat door.

"Got you." Peter grabbed the dog's leash and pulled on it. The dog ignored him and put its nose to the floor and started sniffing.

"What's he doing?" Jessica had entered the fray.

"He's hunting." Peter stared at the very preoccupied hound.

"What?" Jessica looked at me.

"How do I know? I've got a cat around my neck. Get him off me." I tried to pry Muffy's claws from my shirt, but he wasn't giving up his safety perch. He yowled in anger and twitched his tail in front of my nose. "Achoo!"

"Bless you." Peter's automatic response seemed to annoy Muffy. His tail twitched faster.

"This is ridiculous. Here, give me the cat." Jessica reached up and grabbed the oversized fur-ball and pulled.

"Ouch! He's scratching me." I wondered how much blood I'd lost.

"What's the dog looking for?" Peter was obsessed with the sniffing and searching going on.

"I don't know. Throw Muffy out the door." I was cat-free, but Jessica was now the lucky recipient of Muffy's adoration. Her wild-eyed look told me she had a couple of claw marks on her chest. "Here, let me help." Between the two of us we got the cat to the door and he shot off as soon as he saw safety in the tall grasses around the hangar corner.

"He's found something," Peter called out.

Jessica and I exchanged eye-rolls and went back to see what had excited Peter and the dog's interest. If it was a dead rat, I'd personally make sure Peter disposed of it. All this brouhaha was his fault. He let the dog slip out of his hands. I wish the dog had escaped into the surrounding bushes. Then I wouldn't have to deal with Peter and his demands for the flight school logs.

The dog now had its front paws on the metal shelves and was sniffing at the tool boxes and making a big fuss.

"He's a working dog. That's the signal there's something here," Peter said excitedly. He moved the smallest box to one side. "What's this?" He pulled out a small plastic baggie and held it up to show us the white powder in it. The dog barked, froze in place and swished its tail from side to side.

"That wasn't there yesterday when we were messing around with the boards." I stared at the zip lock baggie. It was the same brand they found in my car. I hoped Peter didn't make the same connection. "You were here too, Peter. You didn't see anything like this then, did you?"

I could see by the look Peter gave me he recognized the brand. He opened it up and dipped a finger into the white powder. I'd watched enough CSI programs to know what was coming next. He was going to taste it and declare it as some sort of drug.

I was right. I felt sick at the thought of drugs in Joe's hangar. He couldn't have changed that much since I left him. He'd always been so vocal about his hate for drugs.

The silence stretched on, broken only by the panting of the dog.

"What are you going to do?" This was Jessica, always the practical one. I prayed Peter would decide to do nothing. My prayers were ignored.

"I've got to call Masters. You know that." He fished in his pocket for his phone and came up empty-handed. "It must be in the car. Would you go and get it, Fiona?"

"Why me? I don't want Masters out here." I know I sounded like a spoiled brat. But I really, really couldn't face that man. He would be mad that I hadn't called about the house break-in. And now drugs. I felt that if I could only have time to think things through, I could find out why Joe had to die. And talking to Masters made my head spin. "Give me time to think, Peter, please."

"Fiona, I have to do this. Masters is coming here anyway. Boyd told him about this place being broken into as well. Jessica, would you go get the phone?" Peter's voice had changed from being the puzzled friend into his 'I was once a policeman' tone of authority.

I did not like this new Peter, and it seemed neither did Jessica.

"I think I broke my heel dealing with Muffy. I can't walk properly." Jessica obviously didn't want to deal with Masters either. She slipped off one shoe and examined it closely. "Oops. Come here Fiona and help me with my balance." She swayed dramatically.

Now Jessica could hold the one-legged lotus pose for a long time. I played along and moved to her side. She clutched my shoulder. I was grateful for her stalling tactic, but I knew it wouldn't delay things for long.

Peter glared at us. "Stop stalling both of you. Give me your phone, Fiona."

"Mine's in the office." I said.

"So is mine." Jessica turned her shoe around, carefully looking for any flaws.

"Damn it. Come on dog." He tugged at the hound's leash. It didn't budge.

"Isn't there some sort of order you give it to show its okay to leave the evidence?" Jessica asked.

The giggle that rose in my throat at Jessica's *faux* innocence got quickly stifled at the look on Peter's face.

"You two are in big trouble and you know it." He pulled at the unyielding dog again. "I don't know the order. Go get a phone."

"Let the leash go. The dog's not going to move." This was so obvious; I was surprised Peter was still holding onto it.

"You know I can't leave the scene of the crime in the hands of suspects."

I sucked in my breath at this. "I thought you were my friend, Peter. You're accusing me of being a criminal."

We three stared at each other as the long, accusatory silence, dragged on.

"Hello!" The shout from the door broke our trance. It was the locksmith.

"Great, you're here." Jessica slipped her shoe on and went to greet him.

"So glad you came. We've been waiting for you." I felt the need to act the hostess in the belief that politeness might get rid of the nastiness beside the toolbox. I left Peter, the dog and the drugs in the dim recesses of the hangar and moved towards the sunshine.

"Hey, where you going?" Peter didn't budge from his position, and neither did the dog.

"Outside. The locksmith is going to change the locks on the doors. Then no one but me can get in."

"You can't tamper with evidence of a break in. Wait until after the police have checked it out." Peter heaved a huge sigh of what I could only assume was exasperation.

He was right. I was in enough hot water with Masters over the baggies and the flight records. Plus, I'd already had the house locks changed and hadn't reported that incident to him. I could feel the walls of prison closing in on me.

The locksmith was listening to all this with great interest. "I can wait until the police get here and take pictures. Then change them. I've got nowhere to go."

Except a house full of in-laws. I smiled at him. "How much will it cost extra?"

"An hour won't make any difference." He sounded way too cheerful. And he had reason to. He had a double, or even triple, paying job. He had avoided his in-laws, and he had a great story to regale his buddies with at the diner or bar.

"Can I please have a phone now?" Peter asked.

I decided to play nice and got his from his vehicle. There was something more that Peter didn't know and I couldn't delay admitting to our oversight.

"I left the flight logs at home," I said as I handed him his phone.

"You did what?" I was glad Peter had his hands full with dog leash and phone. He looked like he wanted to throttle me.

"I'm sorry. In the trauma of last night, we forgot them. Don't worry. We changed the locks there. They are safe."

"What trauma. And, what's with all this lock changing?"

Jessica and I exchanged looks. She spoke first. "We had an intruder get into the house last night."

"You what?" Peter slapped both hands on his head, thus jerking the poor hound's leash. The dog growled, but kept his position. "Sorry, boy." Peter looked down at the waiting animal. "I promised Masters I'd bring them to him. And now you tell me you don't have them. And that they are in a house that was broken into. What did the police say?"

"We didn't report it...yet," I whispered.

Peter just shook his head. I was beginning to feel sorry for him. He seemed to have lost all capacity for speech. He took a few deep breaths. "What was taken?"

"Nothing that we could find. The person used a key to get in. It was late. We were tired." As I explained this, I realized how stupid we'd been. If that person had got in with a key the first time, they could have repeated it after we went back to bed.

Peter's ensuing lecture reinforced my feeling of stupidity. The locksmith added his ten cents worth. He said if he'd known that the police hadn't been told and hadn't been guarding the house, he wouldn't have changed the locks. Jessica and I took the tongue lashing very meekly.

Peter ended up his tirade with, "and you've left the flight logs in a house that was broken into. Did you for one moment think that the intruder was looking for them?"

I hadn't thought that. I had no idea what the person was looking for. I did a quick mental run down of the contents of the house. Were the logs still there? Yes, I'm sure they were. "Look, don't worry about it. Jessica and I will go pick them up while you wait here. It's only minutes away." I hoped I sounded contrite enough. "Besides these are just my copies. If someone made off with the originals that means the flight school has a security problem as well."

"I suppose that'd work." Peter sighed. "Hurry and get back before Masters gets over here."

We didn't need any urging to do that!

"Slow down. You don't want to add a speeding ticket to all the trouble you're in." Jessica clutched the armrest.

"You're right. But, I'm hungry. Do you think we have time to grab something to eat?" Most tragedies bring on a lack of appetite. This one tragedy only served to increase mine. I needed to go on a serious diet when all was solved. Then I had a depressing thought. If I ended up in jail, I wouldn't need to go on a diet. I had to find out who wanted Joe dead.

"No, we don't have time. Peter really shouldn't have let you go. He should have made me pick up the things. But he trusts you. He's got the hots for you."

"You're kidding. He's Joe's high school friend."

What's that got to do with it? He never takes his eyes off of you."

Jessica's observation stunned me. I honestly couldn't remember any time I got the impression Peter was in love with me. Mind you, I hadn't ever seen him without Joe in the vicinity—except for the last few days. This revelation put my ownership of the airfield into a new light. What that was, I wasn't sure.

"So that's why he keeps on giving me flying lessons."

"Probably. How many lessons have you had?"

"Actually, not many. But they've spanned a few years. I'm probably his worst student."

"Why do you say that?"

"I can't land. He has to take over at the last minute."

"Remind me not to fly with you." Jessica sounded serious.

"You probably won't ever have to worry about that. I'll never get enough hours to take passengers. I haven't shown up for a lesson in more than six months. And even before I left Joe, I wasn't very consistent about flying time. One tends to forget things when you only have a lesson every month or so. Peter was very patient with me."

"I told you. He's smitten with you. I bet he'd do anything for you."

"Would he kill Joe for me?" The words popped out of my mouth before I had time to think about them.

"What? Didn't you say he was Joe's best friend?"

"He was a high school friend. I'm not sure about the best friend part. Chuck Boyd was closer to Joe. They were out at the airfield together all the time. Peter spent most of his time doing police things. He only started instructing full-time at the airfield after he retired last year."

"We need to make a spreadsheet with all the people who could have sabotaged Joe's airplane and their motives. Let's see...My number one candidate is Balasi. And it's not just because I don't like the look of him. He's too pushy about the business deal. Maria is high on the list. But she is in love with Joe. Then there's that Hasborough Development guy, Arnold. You suggested Peter. Who else?" Jessica leaned back into her car seat and closed her eyes in thought.

"Not Peter. I was wrong to say that. And not Chuck Boyd. I like them both." I knew this was not a rational reason, but I couldn't help it. If I couldn't trust these two, who could I trust? "Anyhow, we don't have time, we're at the house. Run in and get the flight school logs. I'm sure I left them on the kitchen counter. I'll turn the car around and keep the engine running." I jabbed Jessica in the ribs to get her out of her thought process. I was afraid where it might lead to.

Jessica leaped out the car and ran to the house, did a U-turn and came back. "Keys."

I forgot I had the only set of new keys and they were with the car keys. I turned off the ignition and decided to run in with her and use the facilities. Memo to self, cut down on the coffee.

The house phone started ringing as I exited the bathroom.

"Ignore it, we don't have time. I've got the logs and the thumb drive," Jessica said as she ran for the front door. The machine clicked on.

"Why the thumb drive?" I asked, as I slammed the door shut and double locked it.

"It seems safer to keep it close by. And, we have to tell Masters about the contents. Plus, we haven't finished digging." Jessica said as she got into the passenger seat.

"So, why are we telling Masters about it now?"

"I didn't say we'd tell him today. We'll see how things play out when we see him."

I started the engine and we peeled out the driveway. Jessica shot me disapproving look at my speed. I ignored it and we made it back to the hangar in record time.

Peter was standing alone outside. The hound and the locksmith weren't in sight. I supposed Masters and the rest of the squad were inside dusting and doing police things. I was wrong.

"I tried calling you at home. Masters said you were to meet him at the police station. There's nothing more he wants to do here at the moment," Peter explained.

"You mean he didn't search the place?" I was disappointed and a little insulted that my hangar hadn't warranted much time from the police.

"He searched. That bag was the only drug evidence. I paid off your locksmith. Masters doesn't want you to get the locks changed."

"Why not?"

"Evidence." Jessica answered before Peter.

"What if this person uses the key and comes in here again?"

"I'm to stay here and keep an eye on things." Peter squared his shoulders and, I swear, looked very cop like at that moment.

"Can you do that? I mean, you're retired," I asked.

"They're short-handed at the station. Masters deputized me."

"Huh? I didn't know they did that sort of thing nowadays." I looked at Jessica and winked.

"Stop stalling and get over to the police station. That's an order." Peter rolled his eyes.

Now, I really hate the way people do that. It is so juvenile. And, being ordered to do something brings out all the rebellious, teenage traits in me. I was hungry and annoyed. "We're eating lunch first. Then we'll see Masters. He couldn't wait for us. And I'm not waiting lunch for him." I gave Peter the evil eye and went to my car. "Come on, Jessica." But she didn't follow me. I turned to see her and Peter staring at me with their mouths open. Peter said something to her. His voice was so low I couldn't hear a word of it. She shrugged, then came towards me.

"What did Peter say to you?" I asked.

"He said, 'let her enjoy her last meal.' What was that childish display back there all about?" Jessica said this all very quietly.

I burst into tears. "It's just all too much. I don't know what to do next. And now Peter thinks I'm guilty." I sobbed into Jessica's very comforting shoulder.

"It was a joke. We'll get this sorted out. One step at a time, honey. Don't worry." She patted my back as I sniffled into her nice white shirt. "Here, blow your nose."

"I'm still hungry," I wailed. Then, for some reason, I started laughing. I must have made a disgusting picture. Laughing, sniffing, blowing nose and wailing are not a pretty combination.

Jessica burst out laughing. "Look at poor Peter. He is staring at us. He's too scared to come over and find out what is going on."

"Let's get in the car and leave. I can't have him see me like this." I hopped into the nearest seat. Jessica moved around the car and took over driving duties again. I sniffled, blew my nose and generally tried to mop up the results of my breakdown.

"Where are you going?" Jessica was driving to the south side.

"I'm going by Boyd's. I want to get the story of what the police uncovered from him. You never know. All information is valuable." But Boyd's hangar was closed up and no one around. Jessica was understanding the geography of the airfield by now, and she took the south-side track off the field instead of retracing our path to go out via the official access road.

"Look, we don't want to make your situation worse. We'll stop by the police station first. Then we'll eat." Jessica made it all sound very reasonable.

"Alright. It'll make my 'last meal' taste all the better." I gave a little, and maybe slightly hollow, laugh.

The police station was only minutes away. The place was very quiet. There were only two cars in the lot. One civilian and one old squad car that had seen better days. It was a Sunday, but still, crime doesn't stop for the Sabbath. We parked and with flight records in hand, marched up to the front desk. Much to my delight, the desk clerk told us that Masters wasn't on the premises. We could wait if we wanted. He pointed us to the ugly brown and hard chairs lining the wall. I guess he hoped we would wait, if only to alleviate his obvious boredom. He had two completed Sudokus on the desk. He began chatting. "Did you ladies enjoy your dinner last night?"

Jessica's expression was more of a, *what's it to do with you*, than her spoken, "yes, we did."

The clerk must have sensed this, because he elaborated. "I was at the Avernus' place too. I saw you there. Don't you think their cooking is the best? Better than Mama Rosa's any day."

I sucked in a breath when I heard this. But, before I could say anything, Jessica took over.

"Give these papers to Detective Masters. Tell him that Mrs. Tomei and Ms. Feinstein went to get some lunch and that they'll be back later." She smiled sweetly at the man and handed over the sheaf.

"Mrs. Tomei?" He stuttered. "I'm sorry. My apologies." Then he scribbled onto a sticky note and stuck it on the papers.

"Come on Fiona. Let's get lunch." Jessica led the way out of the door.

CHAPTER 14

"I can't believe I ate there!" I pounded on the steering wheel.

"What are you upset about? And you're driving too fast again." Jessica clutched the passenger strap handle.

"The restaurant last night. I didn't know it belonged to Maria's family."

"Well, they didn't seem to mind. And the food was good. They obviously didn't poison it."

"Stop being so reasonable. She's my enemy." I was getting more upset by the minute.

"She wasn't there. And there didn't seem to be any recognition from anyone. Our waiter was very solicitous."

"I guess so. But it still makes me mad I spent my money at her place." I sat and fumed a bit at the stop light. "What kind of food do you want to eat?"

"There are cold cuts and salad in the 'fridge," Jessica answered.

"Salad isn't appealing. Let's eat out. I'm in the mood for comfort food."

"I read an article in the *New York Times* about Italian hot dogs in New Jersey. They sounded wonderfully decadent—fried peppers, onions and potatoes crammed into an Italian roll along with a grilled hot dog. Is there somewhere nearby where we can get one?"

"Oooh yes! They are delicious. There's a *Jimmy Buff's Italian Hot Dogs* just outside town."

THE ITALIAN HOT dogs were all that I remembered. Hot, juicy, greasy and wonderful. We ate in silence, savoring every flavorful mouthful.

"Oh my god, I'd forgotten how great grease tastes. I won't be able to get into those new workout clothes I bought." Jessica slowly licked every one of her fingers then patted her stomach in satisfaction.

I hid a smile behind my last, grease-free napkin. New Jersey food was corrupting my health conscious, Manhattan friend. I wondered what her reaction would be to a typical Jersey breakfast of Taylor Ham, egg and cheese on a hard roll. I'd save that treat for another day. First, we had to figure out why Joe died, and who did it before Masters jumped to the wrong conclusion about me and the NTSB got involved. I didn't know how long the government would be sequestered. I gathered up the pile of greasy, used napkins and paper plates, double-wrapped them in plastic bags, and dusted the crumbs off the picnic table. We were sitting outside on my porch to eat. Jimmy Buff's was full so we'd brought the sandwiches home. The sun was warm and I didn't want the greasy smell in the house. It was bad enough to have it on our breath, but to smell it all night would be horrible. Here at least we could clean our teeth and scrub the grease from our hands.

"I've been thinking about last night's break in here." I finished washing my hands at the kitchen sink. "We talked a lot at the restaurant about the things we found. What if our waiter overheard and reported it back to Maria?"

"Hmmm. That's an idea. But why go to the trouble of coming here?"

"She might not want her smutty emails made public."

"There might be more on the thumb drive that we didn't find. Let's look." Jessica took her turn at the sink. Then, hands grease free, she sat down at the computer and started hunting.

"Look. He downloaded his phone texts." I shunted over to her side of the table and looked on. She was so much better at information gathering than I. Under Jessica's expert fingers it didn't take long to uncover the texts and more emails between Joe and Maria.

The first few emails were all lovey-dovey. Not wanting to dwell on them, I made Jessica scan through them quickly. Then came an interesting one. Maria wanted Joe to bring her cousin in as a consultant. What kind of consultant, she didn't say. But she copied and pasted an email from Balasi to her. It involved the leasing of Joe's hangar and a purchase of a twin-engine airplane. Balasi wanted Maria to buy the twin. She didn't have the money, so she asked Joe for it. The next few emails got a little heated. Joe said he didn't have the money. His divorce (to me) was going to be expensive. *No, it wasn't. We were doing a 'do-it-yourself' kind of divorce, so Joe lied to her.* The next email was forwarded from Balasi. He told Maria he wanted to buy a share in the airfield. Maria added her two bits worth to the end and said that this offer would solve all Joe's problems. He could get his divorce and they could get married. *Hmmmmm? Joe won't sell the airfield.* I didn't understand why Joe had filed these separately from the ones we'd read yesterday. They were older, from the time we split up...and before that.

"These are interesting." Jessica reads faster that I. She pointed to the bottom of the screen. It was a recent one. Sent about a week before Joe was killed. It's an exchange between the lovebirds. Joe writes, 'We need to talk,' Maria answers, 'I'm on a job. What's up?' His reply must have made her crazy. He said, 'Fiona's coming to town next week.' Maria shoots back, 'Tell that bitch to stay away.' He answers, 'No can do. She's my wife.'"

"I wish I could have seen her face when she read that one. What does she say?"

"Oh wow! 'If it's a choice between her and me, you know what you should do.' That sounds like a threat to me." Jessica scrolled down some more. "I'm not sure what this means. Joe answers, 'Things aren't working out.' Then the texts stop."

"Yes, it is a threat. But not enough to kill someone. I'm getting confused. Who have we got on the suspect list?" I hoped my confusion was due to the huge hot dog and fixings lying like a stone in my over-stuffed stomach.

"First on the list is Demetri Balasi. He wanted Joe out the way so he could use the airfield for his drug business."

"I guess that's a good motive. But the developer, Arnold Watson, has a similar motive. Joe didn't want to share his airfield with either of them." I searched in my purse for an antacid while I thought about this. I wondered if Jessica also had indigestion.

"There's your brother-in-law, George. Could he have killed his own brother to get a share of the airfield?"

"I'm not sure. That's really drastic. But he needed the money to put into the restaurant, and a sale to Watson would solve his problems."

"What about Chuck Boyd? He too wanted a part of the airfield." Jessica hesitated when she posited this one.

"Yes, but Chuck went to school with Joe. They were friends." There was no way I could picture Chuck killing anyone.

"How about Maria for a killer?" Jessica mused.

"I'd really like it to be her. But why? It doesn't compute. She was in love with Joe. She was hysterical at the accident scene."

"I hate to say it, but you're the only one with anything like a motive."

I hated Jessica for putting into words my thoughts. "Thanks, I thought you were my friend."

"Don't be silly, of course I am."

"Masters seems to act as if I am guilty."

"Speaking of Masters, we should go there now." Jessica closed down the computer and took the thumb drive out. "We'll take this with us."

"NICE OF YOU two to show up." Masters jerked his thumb towards the inner sanctum of the police station and his office.

I decided to ignore Masters' feeble attempt at sarcasm and smiled brightly at him. "Hope you had as good a lunch as we did. Jimmy Buff's was a special treat for Jessica."

"So that's where you went. I thought I told you not to leave town."

"You said, 'Stick around. Don't go far.' Five miles for a hot dog isn't far." I knew I was pushing his buttons, but I couldn't help myself. The talk Jessica and I had over lunch rattled me, and I get flippant when scared. Jessica jabbed me in the ribs and winked at me.

"Sit down there and there." Masters growled, pointing to two chairs on the one side of a conference table. He waited until we were seated, then took his own chair, opened up a folder, and laid out some sheets on the desk.

"Now, what I want to know is why you, Ms. Tomei, leased your husband's Cessna?"

This shocked me. "I never leased the Cessna. I always flew the Super Cub." I hated the Cessna. It had too many instruments. I got confused watching them all. The Super Cub had the bare minimum. And it floated so gently in the air. The other airplane felt like a flying tank compared to it. "Where did you get this information? Let me see." I reached over the table to pull the sheets towards me.

Masters slapped his hand on his copies. "From the flight school records."

"They didn't say that." I interrupted him.

"They do on my copy." Masters jabbed his finger down on the sheet.

"You have a second copy?" Jessica asked.

Masters was silent for a moment. I could hear the gears clicking in his brain. "Yes. I stopped over at the flight school after checking out your hangar. They found their records. Someone misfiled them."

"Can we see them?" Jessica asked.

Masters ignored her and addressed me. "Why do you say you didn't lease the Cessna when I have it down here?"

"That's not what my copy says. Compare them. I left them at the front desk." I was starting to feel scared now. Everything was pointing to me.

Masters shuffled through his papers. Then reached for the intercom. "Do you have anything that Mrs. Tomei left for me?" The speaker squawked something back at him. "Well get them in here right now."

"While we're waiting for the papers, we'll talk about the illegal substance found in Joseph Tomei's hangar." Masters sat back, folded his arms, and raised his eyebrows in a silent question.

By telepathic mutual consent Jessica and I let the silence drag on. I wasn't about to start defending myself on this charge. I had absolutely nothing to do with the drugs, I didn't even know what kind they were. We stared at Masters.

"Where did you get them from?" He blinked first.

"I didn't get them from anywhere. I never saw them before."

"Are you telling me your husband stored them there?"

"No, Joe hated anything to do with drugs. Anyhow, they weren't there when we moved the shelves to get to Muffy's exit hole."

"Oh, so you're saying you put them there?"

"No, Fiona didn't say that, and you know it," Jessica burst out.

A knock on the door saved us all from a 'he said, she said' argument. The desk clerk entered. He looked a bit sheepish. "Sorry sir, I didn't see you walk in." He handed Masters the papers, with the yellow sticky note still stuck on them.

Masters quickly scanned both sets of records.

"What do you see?" Jessica asked the question on the tip of my tongue.

Masters ignored her.

"What's the big deal with the two copies?" Jessica asked.

"They're different. One shows Mrs. Tomei leasing the Cessna and the other has Demetri Balasi as the person leasing it." Masters turned the papers around and pointed to the lines in question.

"The one you got is a fake. I told you, I never rented the Cessna. Anyhow, what does it matter who rented the Cessna?"

"Have you forgotten that this is the airplane with the drug residue?" Masters asked.

I hadn't forgotten. I remembered every moment of the past four days perfectly. My life was spinning out of control. Every finger was pointed at me. I could feel the tears bubbling up. I breathed deeply. I needed to gain control. I looked at Jessica. *Please help me. Do something.*

"Why don't we all go out to the airfield and check the original against these copies?" God bless her. She gave me some thinking time.

"Good idea." Masters nodded approvingly. And he actually smiled. Wow, I didn't know the man could do anything but look displeased.

Masters stopped to say something to the desk clerk on the way out. Jessica and I got into my car and left the parking lot before Masters had even reached his car.

"I'm stopping by the hangar to get my phone," I said as I turned up the airfield access road. "It'll only take a minute."

"Good idea. Will Peter let us in?" Jessica wondered.

"He can escort us to the office if he thinks we'll contaminate the scene." I hoped he wouldn't make a fuss, but I wanted my phone. I should have got it when Peter and I had that standoff over the phones.

"Oh look. Peter is going into the flight school." Jessica pointed to the disappearing figure.

"I guess he got taken off guard duty." I slowed down. "Damn, he has the keys. We'll have to go in. Quick before Masters pulls up."

"Too late, there's a car coming up the road," Jessica said.

I turned to look at the driver and slid down in my seat. "No. Don't get out. Hide."

"That's the same person who did the donut on the golf buggy." Jessica was still sitting up in her seat. "Why should I hide?"

"Because it is Maria and I don't want to deal with her."

"Don't worry. She's not looking at us. She's going into the flight school."

"What are you two doing?" I hadn't even heard Masters pull up and get out of his car.

"Nothing."

"Well stop doing nothing and get out." He pulled open my door to make sure I complied and ushered us through the flight school front door.

Maria wasn't in sight. The ladies' room would be my guess. I hoped she'd stay in there for a long time. I didn't want a repeat of our last meeting.

"Hi, Mrs. Tomei." It was Jimmy, the new flight dispatcher.

"Hi everyone." Peter emerged from the men's room.

"Who's looking after the hangar?" Masters asked him.

"Chuck Boyd showed up. He's good. I needed the facilities."

I wondered if Peter had deputized Boyd. This small-town, everybody knows everybody else was beginning to aggravate me. I couldn't even go out of town to eat without bumping into my nemesis' relatives. This thought stirred something deep inside me. I should tell Masters and Peter my suspicions of Maria breaking into my house. I opened my mouth to speak when I saw something familiar tucked down by the couch near the ladies' room door.

"This is Joe's laptop case. I recognize the decal." I pulled it out.

"Where did that come from?" Masters asked Jimmy.

"I dunno. I never noticed it before. It is kind or hidden away."

"It's empty." I'd unzipped it and looked inside.

"Is there a laptop around the back there?" Masters indicated to Jimmy to look behind the counter. He shook his head.

"Joe could have left the case behind when he gave the laptop to Boyd.

"We'll ask him in a minute. In the meantime, get me the originals of these flight records." Masters showed Jimmy our two sets.

Jimmy shuffled through some papers. Then he pulled open a file drawer. There was some more rifling through files. He scratched his head. "I can't find the originals. I have a copy here." He lifted it off the counter.

Masters looked at it. "It's the same as mine. When you made a copy for me, what did you use?"

"This one," Jimmy held up the paper in his hand.

"Look very carefully. Is this what you gave Mrs. Tomei?" Master proffered my copy.

"I guess so. They look the same." Jimmy peered closely at both copies. "Oh wait, these lines are different." He pointed to my name and Balasi's.

"We know that. The question is which came from the original." Masters was in full interrogation mode now. "Where did you get the set you made a copy of for Mrs. Tomei?"

"The filing drawer." Poor Jimmy, he was looking scared now.

"Where did you find this copy? Think carefully now." Masters' glare put even more fear on Jimmy's face.

"Ms. Avernus gave it to me."

"Do you know if she's here at the airfield now?" Masters had everyone's attention.

"Yes sir, she is. I saw her come in. I think she's in the ladies' room." Jimmy pointed to the far end of the flight school.

Masters covered the distance very quickly and flung open the door. It was empty.

"How many exits are there to this place?" Masters' frustration was blatant.

"Three. The front door to the parking place. The door to the apron. And the double wide out from the classroom area." Jimmy pointed to the back of the school, past the lady's room.

"Is it usually locked?"

"No. The students use it. There are picnic tables outside."

I knew that. I'd used that door many times. It was the nearest exit to get from the lady's room to Joe's hangar. I'd use them more, if they weren't so heavy and cumbersome. Maria slipping out that way wasn't necessarily a confession of guilt.

Masters ran his fingers through his hair. He must feel as frustrated as I felt. He flipped open his phone. "Send a squad car around to the airfield. Meet me at the Tomei hangar." Then he marched out the front door. Peter followed him to his car. Jessica and I brought up the rear and jumped into my car. We formed a little procession over to the hangar.

"I just know Maria stole the laptop. But why?" I said.

"The emails and texts show Joe wasn't interested in her or her schemes."

"So what? Getting Joe out of the picture wouldn't help her with her schemes."

"Maybe it is revenge," Jessica said.

"Like I said, she was distraught at the accident."

By now we were at the hangar. Masters and Peter were already out of their cars and talking to Boyd. I jumped out in time to hear him say, "The laptop was in its case when Joe left it with me."

"That proves Maria stole it." I was jubilant.

"Maybe. It's all circumstantial," Masters replied.

"Like everything is circumstantial about the evidence you say makes me guilty." I couldn't help myself.

"Calm down. I know you didn't do it," Peter said.

I shot him a grateful look. Maybe Jessica was right, he did have the hots for me.

Masters interrupted my beginnings of thanking Peter. "Let's go in the hangar and look at this crime scene. The squad car is searching the airfield for Maria Avernus. I want to go over what you did in here." He held out his hands for the keys. Boyd dropped them in.

"I'll go meet the squad car and help them find her. I know this airfield and what she looks like." Boyd got into his truck and drove off.

Masters fumbled with the lock. I wanted to snatch the keys from him and show him how you have to jiggle the key, first one way then the other. Jessica sensed my impatience and held onto my arm. "Don't push it," she hissed.

"Stay behind me." Masters stepped over the threshold. The three of us followed him in. "Now show me what you were doing when you found the illegal substances?"

"We were over there, in the back." I pointed and Masters moved towards the shelves.

We followed in silence. Masters shone his flashlight on the shelves. I held my breath and silently prayed that the offending packages had miraculously disappeared. The beam of light played along the shelves, picking out numerous metal toolboxes, spare parts, and other metal objects. Next to a grease-stained cardboard box was the plastic baggie.

The light came to a halt. I leaned forward, mesmerized by the white powder encased in plastic. "I really hoped it was a bad dream," I said.

"Why were you in this area?" Masters asked.

The man door banged shut in the wind and the place got dark before I could answer. "Let me get the lights." I turned towards the switch inconveniently placed on the far wall. But before I could get to it, the door swung open with a crash. I jumped a mile and spun around to look. I saw a flash and heard breaking glass. My first thought was the wind had knocked something over. Then the flash grew into a flame and someone screamed *Fire*. It might have been me.

"Where's the fire extinguisher?" Masters yelled.

"By the door," Peter shouted back and made a run for it. The flames licked across the floor and grew to create a barricade between him, the fire extinguisher, and the door.

"The fire is feeding off the oil on the floor." Peter ran back to us. "Call 911."

It was getting really hot and smoky in the place and I was scared. So was Jessica, judging by the way she clutched my hand. Masters shouted into his phone. Peter picked up a ground cloth and tried to beat the flames back. They just grew and completely blocked our path to either the office or the man door. Jessica and I backed up until we bumped into the metal shelves. My foot kicked something metal and I looked down. It was Muffy's food bowl.

"Muffy. Muffy." I shouted.

"Why are you screaming for the cat?" Peter shouted back.

"His exit hole. It's back here." I pulled at the tool boxes. "Help me."

Jessica understood what I meant and started tugging at the wood covering the hole. "It's stuck. Come on. Pull this wood off. There's a hole behind it." She cried.

"We've got to move the shelves." Peter and Masters pushed us out the way put their weight into pulling the heavily laden shelves away from the wall.

Jessica and I pulled anything we could lay our hands on off the shelves. The heat from the flames got hotter. I looked over my shoulder. Big mistake. All I could see was orange flame. Then a breath of air came from the wall. I saw a sliver of daylight. But the 'emaciated Muffy-sized' opening was too small for any of us. We pried at the plywood, but whatever Peter had used to attach it to the bricks, worked too well. Finally, with one last concentrated effort by the four of us, it came loose. We tumbled backward in a heap and looked up at the sunlight pouring through the hole.

"Come on. Get through it." Masters pushed Jessica and she slid easily through. I was next. I wasn't as thin as my friend, but I made it through. Next came Peter. He was a skinny guy. But poor Masters had a hard time. He got his shoulders out. Then had to ease back in. There was a brief silence, and I could see the flames in the background through the hole. Then his hand appeared and he tossed his gun and holster out. I heard sirens in the distance. *Hurry up.* Masters' head appeared again, then his shoulders. He sucked in his breath and reached out his hands. Jessica took one arm and Peter took the other. They pulled. I grabbed hold of his head and pulled.

"Ouch. Stop it." Masters shook his head. I think I had hold of his ears. Then with a huge grunt, his belly popped loose, Peter and Jessica fell backward and Masters scrambled to his feet. He grabbed his gun and ran around the front of the hangar. We followed suit. The only thing there were our two cars.

The sirens got closer and the fire department came racing up. The pumper and ladder truck screeched to a halt. I couldn't look. All of Joe's dreams were going up in flames. I sank down on the grass beside my car on the side away from the fire. Jessica sat down beside me and put her arms around me.

"What happened?" I whispered.

"It looked and sounded like a Molotov cocktail."

"How do you know what one is?" I looked at my elegant, serene friend in astonishment.

"I watch movies."

That made sense. One of my favorites, Dr. Zhivago, had lots of Molotov cocktails being tossed around.

"Why would someone throw one?" I wondered.

"Maybe to burn the drugs."

That begged the question of who the owner of those drugs was. Jessica and I tossed this around for a while. I was pretty sure the drugs belonged to Balasi. But he wasn't anywhere around. I kept coming back to his cousin, Maria. But why? To make me look guilty. I was just about to voice this to Jessica when the noise of a heavy diesel engine driving away alerted us to the end of the fire-fighting action. I eased my cramped legs and stood up to look over the roof of the car. The pumper was leaving. The fire chief's vehicle was still there, along with a rescue truck and ambulance. And the airfield denizens were huddled together looking at the scene. The hangar doors were wide open. Funny, I hadn't heard them being dragged along their rails. The screaming of metal can usually wake the dead. Jessica stood up beside me and we walked around the car to join the crowd.

"How much damage did the fire do?" I called out to the back of the gawkers. Their heads turned to look.

"You? You're still alive!" The shriek pierced the silence that followed my shout. Maria pulled away from the crowd and ran straight for me. Before I could move, she was on top of me and pulling my hair. "You bitch. You should be dead." She had a fist full of my hair and the pain was excruciating.

"Get her off me." I tried to shake her loose, but she held on tight. I sensed Jessica nearby. I hoped she was whacking Maria.

"Grab her." That was Peter's voice.

"Don't pull her. She's got my hair." I could only imagine the scene. All the able-bodied men pulling Maria off me and my hair with her. I did not want to be bald.

Slowly the pain eased and I was able to look around. Boyd and Masters were trying to hold Maria down. She was flailing around on the ground, screaming nonsense. I heard the words 'Joe, airplane, bitch, dead, fuel' spew out of her. Peter had his arms around me and Jessica was smoothing my cheeks and muttering to herself.

"You did it, didn't you, Maria?" It all became clear to me now. "You were in the flight school when I called in for a lesson. You thought I would be taking the Super Cub up with Peter. You put the water in the fuel. And then you left before Boyd asked Joe to take the banner tow. You killed Joe. But you thought you were killing me."

I remembered the look of horror on her face as I looked through the departing ambulance window. "You knew Joe didn't want to divorce me. And he didn't want to marry you because of your cousin's drug dealings." I was on a roll now. When I stopped talking, the only sound to be heard was Maria's panting. All eyes were riveted on me. I went on. I didn't want to spare this evil woman from any hurt. "What you didn't know was that I wanted the divorce. It was my idea, not Joe's. You didn't have anything to fear from me. But Joe would have found someone else. He always had a roving eye." As I said this, I realized it was true. Even if Joe had begged me on his knees to come back to him, I wouldn't have.

I shrugged off Peter and Jessica's embraces and moved to stand over Maria. I got a whiff of a familiar scent — the one on my bomber jacket. And the same scent lingering in the house. "It was you who broke into my house."

Maria and I locked eyes. I saw hate and evil in them. She spat on the ground. "I put a curse on you. You stole my Joe from me. You should have flown that day. You should be dead. Not him. I curse you, your family, your children, everyone." Two uniformed cops hustled her into the back seat of the squad car and slammed the door. Mercifully shutting off the words that were still coming out of her mouth.

"Let's get you out of here." This was Peter. He steered me towards my car.

"Do these curses really work?" I was shaken by what Maria said and did. How could anyone be that wicked?

"Only if you're Italian and believe in them." Peter pushed me gently into the passenger seat.

"I'm Irish. They believe in curses." I knew I was rambling, but I couldn't stop myself.

"Don't worry about it. She is demented." He buckled me into my seat and took his place at the wheel. I heard the rear door slam and hoped it was Jessica getting in.

"What will Masters say? He'll think I'm escaping."

"Don't worry about it. He'll see you later."

"Oh joy." I gave a rather hysterical giggle.

"She's in shock. She needs some water." Jessica's voice from the back was welcome.

"I need something stronger than water." My voice sounded strange to my ears. "My hair hurts. No, my head hurts. I can't tell the difference. Can hair hurt?"

"She got a hank of it." Peter turned to look at my head.

"Let's go back and get it. I want my hair." I was feeling very woozy now. The sunlight disappeared.

CHAPTER 15

opened my eyes. The daylight outside had that subdued look, like it was evening. I heard voices outside the bedroom door. I strained my ears to catch the words but they were too soft. I sounded like more than two people were out there. I lifted up the bed covers. I was still dressed. Thank goodness for that. I didn't know who put me to bed. Then I remembered Jessica was in residence, so if I were naked, it wouldn't be so bad. Though I didn't want her to see my jelly roll. Then I remembered that same jelly roll trying to squeeze out of Muffy's escape hole and the fire. Where was Muffy? I scrambled out of bed. Was my cat dead? What had happened? I caught sight of myself in the dresser mirror. *My god. I look a fright. What happened to my hair?* The memory started flooding back. I ran into the living room. Boyd, Peter, Jessica and Masters were seated on the sofa and chairs. Beer and wine glasses were arrayed before them. There was even a bowl of popcorn.

"You're having a party without me!"

Jessica jumped up. "No, sweetie. You passed out. We were waiting for you. See, we've only had one drink each. What do you want?"

"Whatever you're having." I sat down in her vacated seat and reached for her glass and took a drink. "What happened?"

"Sweetie, Maria confessed." Jessica took another glass and poured herself some wine.

"Well, duh. After that performance it was obvious she set the fire."

"No, not just to the fire. Also to killing Joe. You're off the hook." Jessica raised her glass in a toast.

"I know. I figured it out. Didn't you hear me? She wanted me dead. She loved him. She put a curse on me. How can anyone be that evil?" I searched their faces for an answer.

Masters took over from Jessica. "Like you said, Maria was in the flight office when you called to book the lesson with Peter. So was Joe. He said he'd prep his Super Cub for you as you liked flying it better than the Cessna. This incensed Maria, and, according to Jimmy, she berated Joe and accused him of wanting to get back with you. Apparently, he didn't deny it strongly enough for Maria. Anyhow, he pulled the Super Cub out and pre-flighted it. Then went for breakfast. Maria took this opportunity to put water in a plastic bag and insert it into the fuel tank. I'm told that the plastic will melt in an hour or so, and the water will stop the engine. Maria then left the airfield for a hair appointment. She wasn't around when Boyd's airplane malfunctioned, and Joe took the banner tow in his Super Cub. That's why she was so shocked at the accident scene. She thought she'd be crying crocodile tears over you Fiona."

"And me," Peter added. "I was supposed to be in that airplane too."

"What about the drugs in Joe's hangar? Who planted them?" I didn't want to dwell on the horror of death.

"We believe it was Maria, with some help from her cousin Balasi. We haven't tracked him down yet. But we did find the originals of the flight records. Someone had doctored them. My theory is that Balasi wanted the airfield to further his drug operation. He was already moving small amounts in. Hence the remnants in the Cessna. If you were out of the picture. He figured he could get his hands on the airfield. They wanted the laptop and thumb drive to destroy all evidence of Balasi wanting the airfield. That's why Maria broke into your house."

"So Hasborough had nothing to do with all this?" I was kind of sorry. I wanted George and his buddy Arnold to be guilty of something.

"There's nothing obvious on that front. But who knows what we'll uncover. There's still a lot of investigating to do."

"What happens next?" I wasn't sure I wanted an answer. But I had to ask.

Masters didn't answer this one. I looked at the other three. Two of Joe's best friends and my best friend.

Peter took up the challenge. "You've got an airfield to run. I'll help you."

"Me too." Boyd chimed in.

"Tomorrow we'll talk to your lawyer and see what we can do about buying back the tax liens from your brother-in-law," Jessica added. "We can save this airfield. You do want to save it, don't you?"

"Yes, I do. Very much."

"To the Airfield, Under New Management." Peter and Boyd almost said this in unison. We raised our glasses in a toast. Even Masters joined in. He was quite a nice cop once he thought a person was innocent.

The End

ABOUT THE AUTHOR

Welsh-born Penny Thomas spent her first few decades in Egypt, Portugal, Lebanon, and the United Arab Emirates. Then, a stroke of luck took her to the United States of America. Life in New York City and a love of small airplanes provided her with a multitude of plot lines to indulge in her passion for writing fiction. She now enjoys retirement in The Villages, FL. Penny holds a B.S. from Pace University, New York, NY, and an M.F.A. from Seton Hill University, Greensburg, PA. Her novel, *As the Prop Turns*, won Mystery Writers of America, Florida Chapter's *Freddie Award for Writing Excellence*.

9 781962 326094